You Bet Your Life

A Willows Bend Cozy Mystery - Book 1

Evelyn Cullet

Amazon KDP

Published by Evelyn Cullet 2018

ISBN 9781983902956

Typesetting services by BOOKOW.COM

To my Aunt Julia, a real character in her time, and the inspiration for this mystery series. Although she's no longer with us, she'll always be remembered. I'd like to thank my niece and nephew, Christine and George Talan, for allowing me to use their names in this series.

Acknowledgments

Book Cover Designed by Heather Upchurch

Editor: Erynn Newman, A Little Red Inc.

Chapter 1

HEATHER Stanton leaned back in her seat, her head against the cushion, as she glanced out the window at a seemingly endless parade of dismal streets and suburban houses. The hypnotic scenery and gentle motion of the train were mild distractions but did nothing to calm her uneasiness.

In her first-class compartment, she sat motionless and bit her bottom lip, trying hard to keep the tears from her eyes. For the first time in her life, she'd allowed herself to be swept away—like a leaf in the wind. Swept away by emotions, to the point of doing something incredibly irrational and selfish.

Had she lost her mind? She had to have—to abruptly quit her job this afternoon. The very job she'd fought so hard to get two years ago. She'd always considered herself to be non-confrontational, cool and self-sufficient. But when she did lose her self-control, she lost it completely.

And then there was that incident with Jack when she got home. The thought of it twisted her heart until she almost couldn't breathe. She closed her eyes, trying to suppress the ache.

At times, she wanted to jump off the train and go back to Chicago, to her old job and the false security of Jack's arms. But the same determination that made her run wouldn't allow her to. The die was cast. It was too late.

At the sudden tug of the train, Heather jerked forward in her seat and opened her eyes. They'd stopped at a deserted-looking station. The small one-story, slate gray building with weathered shingles, held a single ticket window, the black shade drawn. She groaned at having booked a train that stopped in every small town along the way. It was going to take forever to get to Champaign.

Her cell vibrated. She turned it off. Too many messages she didn't want to read... or answer.

In the window, she caught a fleeting but familiar impression of a woman passing by and had to crane her neck to get a better look. *Aunt Julia?*

She hadn't seen Julia Fairchild in over five years. This woman appeared much older, yet there was the same eight-year age gap between her mom and Julia as there was between herself and her elder sister, Emily.

What would Aunt Julia be doing on this train? The last she'd heard, her mother's younger sister was...

The loudspeaker crackled, interrupting her thoughts. "Attention passengers. The railway tracks a few miles ahead have become unstable, and this train has to be rerouted. If you're traveling to Champaign or beyond, you'll have to get off here at Willows Bend. Keep your tickets. You can either get a refund or catch the next train, which is scheduled to stop here tomorrow night. The railway has made arrangements for you to stay at the Franklin House Hotel as their guest. Sorry for the inconvenience."

Heather let out a breath of frustration. *Perfect.* This was exactly her luck. She really needed some face-time with Emily tonight.

Her older sister was the only person she could or would confide in. Or rather, get reassurances she'd done the right thing. Knowing the level-headed person she was, Emily would probably talk her into taking the next train home to confront her boss—and Jack.

Dread clutched Heather's throat as the tears she'd been suppressing nearly made it to her eyes. She grabbed the handle of her suitcase and stood in line to exit the train.

She'd be okay. She just needed time to ride this out. *That's all I need, just a few more hours. One extra day to let the events of this afternoon settle so I can think rationally again.*

Maybe this rail track problem wasn't such a bad thing after all.

Chapter 2

HEATHER sipped her after-dinner coffee as she peered across the Franklin House Hotel dining room at the woman who resembled her aunt. She'd always adored Julia. In fact, everyone was crazy about her. As a young woman, she'd been daring, charming, and absolutely lovely. Funny to think this somewhat overweight, untidy person might be her. And that bright orange hair. Her aunt would never...

The woman stood, and with an ingratiating twist of the body, she bustled toward the door making an abrupt stop at Heather's table. "Well, for heaven's sake," she said. "If it isn't my favorite niece. I didn't know you were here."

Heather jumped from her seat to give her aunt a hug. "I thought that might be you, but I wasn't sure. It's been a while. You've changed so much." She pulled out a chair. "Sit down so we can catch up."

"You look good, Heather."

"So do you," she lied.

Julia made herself comfortable in the chair across from her niece. "I haven't been invited to any weddings lately, so I'm assuming you're still single."

Heather cringed. She didn't want to talk about her failed love life right now. Especially to her aunt. "Actually, I've been dating a lawyer for the past year. You know him—Jack Steele. He's definitely *not* Mr. Right."

"Sometimes you just have to take a chance. I thought I'd found the right man in my Stanley, nevertheless I ended up leaving him."

Heather couldn't hide her disapproval. "That was a shame. You two seemed made for each other."

"Things just didn't work out. I knew he'd be okay. Not long after we divorced, he married a really nice woman, more suited to him. He still emails me, mostly around the holidays, just to keep in touch. Nice gesture on his part, don't you think?"

Heather didn't answer. She was too full of conflicting thoughts about her aunt. She'd heard through the family grapevine that Julia had made an unsuccessful attempt to rid herself of Stan when they were married by shoving him down the basement stairs. Of course, this was only an unsubstantiated rumor perpetuated by her mother who had always been jealous of her younger sister.

After a moment of uncomfortable silence, Julia continued. "When you said you didn't think Jack was Mr. Right, it just goes to show how people get things wrong. Some family members have gotten it into their heads the reason you've never married is because you're... umm. I don't know how to put this so you won't be offended, so I'll just come out and say it. Because you're not a warm person. Of course, I've never thought of you that way."

Heather never thought of herself that way either. It's just that she didn't like to get close to people—they inevitably disappointed her. But she supposed that's what she must have seemed like to those family members who didn't understand her and probably never would.

When I divorced Stan," Julia continued, "your boyfriend represented me. I found Jack extraordinarily kind, really understanding."

"That's Jack all over." Heather couldn't hide the sarcasm in her voice.

"If I remember correctly, he was pretty much a ladies' man."

A flush of heat hit Heather's cheeks. She opened her mouth to deny it just as a thought slipped across her mind. Was his infidelity that obvious to everyone, but her?

Julia gestured to the waiter for coffee. "You must think I'm a horrid woman for saying that about Jack. My heart has always been my undoing. I've been far too fond of men just like him. Strange isn't it? After Stan, there was a short stint with Roger, and he was bad—though terribly good-looking, and of course, Henry, who I was genuinely fond of, in my own way." Julia tapped the table with her short, unpolished fingernails. "And just to set the record straight, that incident with Henry had absolutely nothing to do with me. It happened months after I'd left him."

Heather was almost afraid to ask. Her curiosity got the best of her. "Incident?"

"Sleeping pills and alcohol. He never recovered." She must have caught sight of Heather's startled expression. "Sorry if I've shocked you."

"I'm not shocked. I'm just... Well, I am, a little."

The waiter brought a cup of coffee to their table and set it in front of Julia, interrupting an unpleasant topic.

Heather pasted on a smile. "I, um. What I really mean to say," she added awkwardly, "is that I'm sorry."

"About Henry?" Julia seemed amused by the idea. "Kind of you, but don't waste your sympathy on me." She stared at her cup for a few seconds in quiet contemplation. "I've really made a mess of my life, haven't I?"

Trying to steer the conversation away from her aunt's feelings, Heather asked, "What happened to you after that?"

"I decided I wanted to see something of the world." Julia's mouth gave a humorous twist. "And now I've seen it." Her amber eyes rotated toward the ceiling. "Maybe a little too much of it."

Heather finally asked the question that had been at the back of her mind. "How did you end up in this backwater town?"

"Same as you. The train."

"Where were you going?"

"Champaign." Julia's head turned to the side as if a thought had just crossed her mind. "Is that where you were going, too?"

Heather nodded as her heart sank. While she didn't mind taking her aunt on as a traveling companion, she didn't know what Aunt Julia planned to do when she got there. She didn't know what *she'd* do either, other than have a talk with Emily.

Julia's mouth twitched. "Your sister got me an interview for a hostess job at a swanky restaurant and dibs on a very nice apartment."

Heather let out a sigh of relief. "How wonderful for you. I'm glad."

"Always the diplomat, aren't you? You must be thankful I'm not dumping myself on you or your sister. Don't deny it. I know what I've become—loud, pushy, and uncouth. Well, there are worse things."

Heather doubted there were,. She'd never admit that to her aunt. What she could do was help her. Putting her own problems aside for the moment, she said, "Since we're both going to Champaign, we could cash in our train tickets and rent a car. I can drive us there in a few hours, instead of having to wait for the next train tomorrow."

"Thanks, I'd like that. But let's wait until morning. There's something important I have to do tonight."

A short man, around sixty with thick gray hair the same color as his wrinkled summer suit, walked toward them. He stopped at their table and pushed his black, horn-rimmed glasses up on his nose. "Julia, my dear. Don't forget about our date."

Her aunt's lips curved into a warm smile. "I won't. I'll meet you in the lobby right after I finish my coffee."

The man gave a satisfied grunt, glanced at Heather, and acknowledged her with a tilt of his head a moment before he made his way out the door.

Heather stared at him as he walked away. "Who was that?"

"Oh, just someone I met in the dining car. Nikos Stamos. As it turns out, we have lots and lots in common. He lives in this town."

"It's funny. I didn't see either of you on the train."

"That's because you were probably in first class. We both traveled coach. It's much cheaper, you get there just as fast, and you meet such interesting people."

A young man wearing a white, summer shirt tucked into tight jeans stopped at their table, his cool, blue eyes assessing Julia's appearance. The man's full lips curved slightly, as if he was about to break into a huge smile. "Gladys?"

Julia turned her head toward the windows. "Sorry, no. You must have me mixed up with someone else."

The young man continued to give her the once-over. "I'm sorry to have bothered you, but you look so much like my cousin, I could have sworn you were her."

Julia waved him off. "It's all right."

He turned in Heather's direction and broke into a smile. "Hello."

She couldn't help smiling back. *What a great-looking guy*. Her gaze followed him as he walked away—admiring his easy, confident walk and the way his muscles moved under that shirt.

Julia opened the forest green handbag in her lap, pulled out a gun, and slammed it down on the table. "Don't worry. He won't bother us again."

Chapter 3

HEATHER threw her napkin over the gun. "Are you crazy?" she whispered fiercely. "You can't pull out a gun and put it on the table while we're having coffee. She shoved the napkin in her aunt's direction. "Put it away. It makes me nervous."

Julia clasped a reluctant hand over the napkin. "Nervous? It makes me feel safe." She picked it up in one flawless maneuver and dropped it back into her purse.

"That guy looked all right to me," Heather said. "Why did you immediately think the worst of him?"

"Because, in my experience, the worst is so often true. Listen, I've been around and seen certain things. Things that would curl that lovely, auburn hair of yours."

"Is that why you bought a gun?"

"I didn't buy it. Stan gave it to me. I told you he was thoughtful." Glancing toward the lobby, she downed whatever was left in her coffee cup. "Well," she said. "I've got to be going. I'll meet you in your room tomorrow morning. What's your room number?"

"Three eleven."

Julia glanced toward the lobby again. "Not too early, though. I may be out late tonight." She opened her purse, pulled out a pack of tiny peppermints and popped one in her mouth. She offered one to Heather, who took the mint and shoved it into the side pocket of her purse.

After her aunt left, Heather finished her coffee and paid the bill. She intended to go to upstairs. What she really needed was a walk to clear her head. Julia's life wasn't the only one that was a mess right now.

She made her way toward the block of boutiques in the town square. Very few people walked the streets. It was only seven on a Friday night, but most of the stores were already closed.

The warm evening breeze brushing her cheeks and gently blowing through her hair refreshed her spirit. She took a deep, cleansing breath. Freedom from everything that had been weighing on her shoulders was liberating, short-lived as the feeling might be.

Turning a corner, she came to a homemade fudge shop. The *Open* sign invited her to walk in. Just a single, small piece would satisfy her craving for chocolate, or maybe two—one for later. She sauntered in and strode along the store's short counter, eyeing the delicious-looking confections. Someone bumped her arm, making her stagger a few steps back.

"I'm sorry," a masculine voice said.

She looked up at the sky blue eyes with their long lashes, the perfectly shaped lips, and the straight nose of the man who had approached their table at the restaurant.

"Oh, it's you," she said.

"Have a sweet tooth, too?"

"Somewhat. But I don't like to overindulge." She'd been trying to lose the extra pounds she'd put on since she moved in with Jack a few months ago.

An attractive, buxom blonde appeared behind the counter and bared her straight, white teeth. "What can I get for you today, Chad?"

He chose a half pound of dark chocolate fudge with walnuts.

She glanced at Heather. "And for you?"

"I'll have the same. Only two pieces though."

"Are you new in town?" he asked as he paid for his purchase. "I don't think I've seen you around before."

"I'm just passing through on my way to..." She probably shouldn't tell him where she was going. "Um ... to visit my sister, a little further downstate."

"Pity you aren't staying." He checked his watch. "It was nice meeting you..."

"Heather."

"Heather," he repeated as though he didn't want to forget it. "I'm Chad Willows."

She grinned as he left the shop. After paying, she followed him out and watched as he walked down the block. He seemed like a nice guy. And hot enough to melt steel.

A couple, walking hand-in-hand on the opposite side of the street, caught Heather's attention. Her aunt and the gray-haired man from the dining room turned into a building with dilapidated aluminum siding. A small, round sign, aged to a dark gray from the weather, hung above the door. In the center of the sign was an image of a black horse running, and underneath it were the words, *Off-Track Betting.*

Heather almost felt sorry for her aunt. Yes, Julia had had an unfortunate life, but the whole thing seemed such a needless waste since she'd grown up with every advantage.

"Poor Aunt Julia—the wrong men and horse racing." Would she ever learn?

Chapter 4

AFTER walking a few blocks, Heather came to a small park near a neat row of bungalows similar to the one she grew up in on the south side of Chicago. A rugged stone bridge stood over a lagoon where two mallards, followed by five ducklings, drifted toward the opposite shore.

Low branches on the weeping willows caressed the ground as they waved in the evening breeze, bidding her to join them. She set herself down on a black, wrought-iron scrolled bench and watched the ducks crossing the water. *Jack would love it here.*

The look he gave just before she fled his apartment haunted her—a long sad look, and something else, maybe a last faint flicker of hope she wouldn't go. They'd spent so many lovely evenings together, she missed the feeling of closeness.

The woman could have been a client, and the kisses might have only been a grateful gesture for all the work he'd done, like he insisted.

Heather pulled out her cell phone and tapped his number. Maybe she'd give him one more chance. Her heart raced as she waited.

"Hello... Hello," a sweet, young voice answered.

She ended the call and dropped the phone in her purse. Not what she wanted to do, but better than insisting she talk to Jack. No way could she win a fight with him—not when lying came as easy as breathing. And Jack Steele was a damn convincing litigator.

Heather opened her bag of fudge and downed one piece followed by the other. They did nothing to soothe the ache in her heart. Now she was sorry she hadn't bought more. Injured, miserable, and yearning for sympathy, she shot to her feet and walked toward the lagoon, her shoes crunching on the small pebbles along the shore.

She picked up a handful. Sifting through the stones, she chose the largest and flung it with every ounce of force she could muster as her head filled with thoughts of Jack and his clients. Mostly women. Rich, good-looking women who were lonely and needed someone to talk to or a shoulder to cry on, both of which Jack was happy to provide.

He said he loved her because she was so simple and uncomplicated. *Uncomplicated? Me?* If he only knew she'd been fooling herself for a long time. The fire that once raged between them had died out months ago. Now there was only the occasional smoldering ember when they'd make up after a fight over something he'd done that he later convinced her was only in her imagination. She'd known better, but she'd always taken him back.

"Hey, take it easy with those stones. You'll hit a mallard."

Heather jumped. In her angry, jealous haze, she hadn't noticed anyone nearby. The heat of embarrassment warmed her cheeks. Her hand trembled as she dropped the few pebbles she had left. "I wasn't aiming at them."

"What were you aiming at?"

Her gaze skimmed the ground. "A ghost from my past," she mumbled and swung around to face the man standing behind her. "Chad, right?" She glanced at the trees. "Willows?"

He nodded, and a loose curl dropped down on his forehead. "Hi Heather."

"Where did you come from?" she asked. "The way you checked your watch in the fudge shop, I thought you might be late for... something."

"I was. It got cancelled. That's what I get for not checking my text messages before I left. So I took a shortcut home and spotted you here."

She glanced at the light ripples on the water as the evening breeze flared the branches of the willow trees. "It's a lovely spot. So serene." *If only my life could be like this.*

"It's one of my favorite places to be on an evening like this. Especially with a lovely woman like you."

How could he know what kind of woman she was? They'd just met. She bit her bottom lip to stop herself from stating the obvious. So why was her stomach fluttering?

"If you don't mind my asking," he said. "Who was that lady you were with at the hotel restaurant?"

"Why?"

"The two of you looked so incongruous sitting together. You in your obviously designer clothes and her looking like she'd just escaped from a gypsy camp."

"That's my Aunt Julia."

"She reminded me so much of my cousin."

"Guess there's someone like her in every family."

He chuckled as if he understood. "Do you have anything planned for this evening?"

She cast her eyes down. "Just thought I'd stroll along the lagoon for a while, and then go back to my hotel room."

"Why don't you let me show you around town?"

It certainly beat sitting in a stuffy hotel room with nothing to watch on television and going to bed. At least her aunt was out enjoying herself, albeit it at a dive where she was probably losing badly on the horses. Maybe she'd better check into that before Aunt Julia lost all her money.

"Come to think of it," Heather glanced up at him. "There *is* one place in this town I'd like to visit."

"I'd be happy to take you. Where would you like to go?"

"The off-track betting parlor."

His eyes widened. "Why do you want to go there?"

"I've always had a weakness for horses. And I saw my aunt go in earlier."

"I understand." He bent his head back. "As a matter of fact, I've got a weakness for horses myself."

***

Chad opened the weather-worn oak door of the OTB parlor, and Heather walked in to inhale the thick air—a mixture of old cigar smoke, men's cologne, burgers, and pizza.

Except for the handsome, blond bartender, it was mostly older men wearing shorts and polo shirts—

some with clothes that looked like they'd been worn more than once in the past few days. The tattoos they sported had to be at least half a century old, inked back when they signified more than mere stylishness.

Chad put a hand on the small of her back and moved her toward the horseshoe-shaped bar as she studied the other customers.

They all had that look—the look of a horseplayer. She'd seen it before, in her aunt's friends and associates. The man next to her reeled off a string of horse racing jargon to another sitting beside him. She had no idea what any of it meant.

"Do you see your aunt?" Chad asked.

"Not yet. She won't be hard to find in this crowd."

The facility looked clean, but it could have used a better air filtration system. The restaurant area had a series of tables, each with its own personal television set. The screens listed the race horse names and the odds. Smaller ones had races going on. All simultaneously.

Heather glanced up to view the six television screens above the bar. "How can anyone concentrate with all this going on?"

"Practice, I guess. How about a drink?"

After today, I could use one. "I'll have a glass of white wine."

She took a seat on a bar stool as Chad placed their orders. "Hey, Derek. A glass of Chardonnay for the lady, and I'll have a Miller Lite."

"You got it, Buddy. Glad to see you're back in town. What's it been, five years?"

"Just about that. Happy to be back."

"Sorry about your sister's accident."

Chad gave him a short nod to acknowledge his concern. "This is Heather."

"Hi. Great to meetcha." Tall, blond, and as muscular as an athlete, Derek was the kind of man who could set a woman's heart fluttering just by smiling at her.

"Nice to meet you, too." She turned to Chad as Derek went to pour their drinks. "Your friend seems very nice."

"Yeah, he's great. We were buddies in school."

She'd lost touch with her school friends when she'd met Jack. Now all her friends were his. He'd made sure of that. So there was no one she could talk to without word getting back to him.

Derek set a glass of wine and Chad's beer on the counter.

"When do you close?" Heather asked him.

"Ten."

Heather checked her phone. "It's nine thirty. So I guess most of the die-hard gamblers have probably left. I'm looking for my aunt. A lady in her mid-fifties, with flaming red hair."

Derek crossed his muscular arms and leaned on the counter. "Yeah. There was a woman like that here earlier, with Nikos. They had an argument and she stormed out."

"Would that be, Nikos Stamos?"

Chad nodded. "This is his place. Big-time gambler. Basically harmless."

A cynical inner voice cut through her thoughts. What did *basically harmless* mean? "My aunt has a penchant for men like Nikos. I'm sure she can take care of herself."

"Since I don't know her, I'll have to take your word." Chad's gaze roved the rectangular room, like he was looking for someone. His lips curved into a teasing smile. This time he looked as though he was smiling at something she didn't see.

She stared at him across the sheen of old oak—so handsome and broad-shouldered. *Too bad I have to leave tomorrow.*

He tipped his head to one side. "Somehow, you don't look comfortable here." He had a disquieting way of looking at her, as though he wondered what her motives really were.

Heather toyed with her glass before taking a long sip of wine. "I don't usually frequent places like this." She put a hand to her mouth and coughed at the thick air.

"Have you ever placed a bet on a horserace?"

"Sure. I went to the Arlington Park Racetrack with friends. Once. I placed bets on some of the races. I don't really know much about horseracing. Guess I was just lucky to have picked a couple of winning horses that day."

His firm mouth curled as if he was on the edge of laughter. "Horseracing isn't like playing the slots. It's not a crapshoot. You figure how the horse has done recently, the bloodline, who the jockey is, the other horses he'll be racing against, and the odds. Always the odds. There's no luck involved at all."

"Thanks. I'll remember that if I ever place a bet again."

"So you lied about being a gambler?"

She crossed her arms. "Actually, I just wanted to check up on my aunt."

"That's what I thought." He tossed some bills on the bar. "Let's get out of here."

The shades of evening had darkened into a clear, starry night as they strolled the three blocks to her hotel and lingered on the sidewalk just outside the door.

"It was nice meeting you," Heather said. "And thanks for going with me to Nikos's place to look for my aunt."

There was a firm strength about his hand as he shook hers. "Are you sure you have to leave tomorrow?"

"Yes. My aunt and I are driving to my sister's in the morning. And she's starting a new job on Monday." Heather slipped her hand from his. still feeling its warmth.

"Well, if you're ever in Willows Bend again, be sure to look me up." He pulled a business card from his shirt pocket and handed it to her.

She read the card. *Willow in The Wind Bookstore.* "What an adorable name. You must be one of the last independent bookstores around."

"I guess we are. My sister and I inherited the place from our grandfather. I recently moved back to help her with it. Guess I'm just a small town guy at heart."

"I'm a big city girl, born and raised on the south side of Chicago. I don't think I could live in a small town. A little too laid-back for me. But it really is very nice here." She checked her watch. "It's getting late, and I've got a long drive ahead of me in the morning."

Chad smiled. "Goodbye, Heather. Have a safe trip."

A mellow glow flowed through her as she turned away and entered the hotel lobby. It was something she hadn't felt in a very long time.

On her way to the elevator, a loud, angry, shrill from an all-too-familiar voice stopped her. The voice came from the direction of the hotel bar. Even with the glass door closed, there was no mistaking her aunt's not-so-dulcet tones.

"This is *not* over! Don't think you're gonna get away with this, you cheating son-of-a no good, rotten… argh!"

Julia swung the door open and hustled past Heather, heading toward the elevator. She pounded the up button several times in rapid succession. Before Heather could reach her, she dashed to the door of the stairwell and ran in.

"Aunt Julia," Heather called after her.

No response. Her aunt must not have heard. She should go after her. Tomorrow morning was soon enough to hear the sordid details, and from the way her aunt sounded, they *would* be sordid.

In her hotel room, Heather grabbed her night shirt and some toiletries out of her suitcase and got ready for bed, ignoring the dozens of messages on her cell phone and the numerous emails on her laptop.

The realization of what had happened at the office that afternoon finally sank in. How could her boss, a man she trusted, turn the tables and make it appear as if she was instrumental in losing a million dollar account? She should have stayed and fought the accusation, but with budget cuts and department consolidations, the never-ending pile of work on her desk had pressed on her psyche until she couldn't think straight, and she finally exploded. Even *her* iron-will cracked when pushed to the breaking point.

Heather climbed into bed, and turned on the television in an effort to put what happened out of her mind. Mulling over her situation was useless. It wasn't going to change anything.

Switching channels, she found an old mystery movie and lost herself in the story for a few minutes, until her aunt's words flashed through her mind and distracted her. Something was up with Julia. Something bad. Heather didn't need to take on Julia's problems right now. She had enough of her own.

Chapter 5

A banging on the door jerked Heather awake. Heart racing, she threw her covers off and jumped out of bed as the morning sunlight filtered in around the heavy light-blocking curtains. The television was still on, so she clicked it off and hurried to see who it was.

Aunt Julia's face stared at her from the other side of the peephole. Heather opened the door as relief slowed her heartbeat.

"Aren't you ready to leave yet?" Her aunt bustled into the room, dragging her suitcase behind.

Heather rubbed the sleep from her eyes and yawned. "What time is it?"

"Nearly eight."

"It's Saturday. You could have waited another hour to wake me. Checkout isn't until ten."

"I want to get on the road before traffic gets bad. You know how jammed the expressways always are."

"Yes, but..."

"But nothing. Please get dressed."

Heather rummaged though her suitcase and grabbed some clothes. She took a quick shower and rushed to dress. Walking out of the bathroom fifteen minutes later, she found her aunt had already packed her night shirt and her laptop and was dragging her suitcase toward the door.

"Wait a minute." Heather threw the rest of her things into her overnight bag and zipped it shut. "Why are you in such a hurry?"

When Julia didn't answer, Heather stepped in front of her before she could take another step. "Okay. What's wrong?"

Dragging her hands over her face, Julia whispered, "Nikos is dead."

Heather shook her head to clear it. Was she hearing things? "What?"

"I said Nikos is dead. Now let's get out of here."

"Well, I'm sorry he's dead, but—"

Julia put a hand up. "You're going to be a lot sorrier when I tell you the circumstances."

Heather wasn't sure if she wanted to hear what they were. She forged ahead. "Just slow down and tell me what's going on."

Julia slumped down onto the bed. "I don't know how it happened. I don't remember doing it. I think I might have killed him. And now I have to get out of town before the cops find his body."

Staggering back a few steps, Heather dropped into the desk chair. "You… you're not serious."

Julia raised and lowered her shoulders. "Come on. I'll show you."

They left their suitcases in Heather's room and walked down the hall to Julia's. She pushed her key card in and opened the door. The room was quiet, as though nothing had happened to break its peaceful serenity, except the early morning chatter of birds outside.

They walked into a macabre scene. Nikos Stamos lay on the bed, head propped up on a pillow stained with blood and possibly particles of his brain. His eyes were open, staring, and there was a bullet hole in his forehead. The beige wool blanket from the bed had been pulled up to his chin.

"Oh, my God!" Heather closed her eyes. But the image was burned into her mind. She pulled her arms close to her body, careful not to touch anything. She didn't want to leave any evidence she was ever there.

Julia stood frozen near the bed. "Just think of how I felt when I woke up this morning and found him like that. I was shocked because I don't know how he got in here. I certainly didn't invite him."

This sounded like an impossible situation. "If you were sleeping next to him, how could you not have heard the gunshot?"

Julia shivered as if it had just sunk in. "It's a good thing I was out cold. I don't remember much about last night after I had that drink. And there's this..." Julia pointed to the cushion on the sofa—its stuffing scattered all over the floor. A convenient silencer.

"Why didn't you call the police?"

"I panicked, packed my bags, and ran to your room to wake you up so we could get the heck outta here."

Heather grabbed her aunt's arm and backed them both out the door. "We need to leave this room. Now!"

In her own room, Heather dropped down into the desk chair again. She closed her eyes and ran her fingers over her forehead to gather her thoughts. "What were you two arguing about in the bar last night?"

Julia paced. "Nikos owns the off-track betting place. Well, he owned it. I asked him to place my bet on a long-shot to win, but he said I didn't win because he'd heard from a reliable source that the horse was going to get scratched at the last minute, so he bet the money on another horse. I'm sure he was lying, because my horse was in the race, and she won." Julia's eyes held a scared rabbit expression. "I need those winnings. They're all I have in the world. Now I'll have nowhere to live and no money for food."

"How could you be so sure *your* horse was going to win the race?"

"The horse's owner and I are old friends. We met at the track recently, and one thing led to another. He told me in confidence, kind of between the sheets, to bet on his horse because she's better than anyone realizes. He's been holding her back, waiting for the right race. For this one, he told the jockey to let the horse go. And sure enough, she won. The odds were forty to one."

"You could give Nikos the benefit of the doubt. Maybe he *didn't* bet your money on the winning horse."

Julia shook her index finger in the air. "Oh, that cheat placed the bet all right. I watched him from the bar."

"How much did you have to drink before you passed out?"

"Just the one glass of wine."

"If you were out cold after that, and you don't remember anything about what happened last night, all I can think of is that you must have been drugged."

"Oh yeah. I'm sure I was because I have a heck of a hangover this morning. I probably got the wine from the same person who killed Nikos." Julia gasped. "Whoever it is must have my money or the winning ticket, or he knows where either one is."

"That stands to reason. Do you have any idea who that might be, someone you met on the train or at the OTB place?"

Julia huffed out a decided, "No."

"What's the last thing you remember?"

"Well, the argument started at Nikos's place right after the race. It got pretty heated as you can imagine. I ended up throwing my wine in his face and ran out of there. By the time I got back to the hotel, I was livid, so I stopped in the bar for a drink to calm down. Nikos must have been right on my heels, because I hadn't even taken a sip before he came in, and the argument continued. I knew I couldn't win it, so I threatened that crook and left.

"I dashed to my room to try to figure out how I was going to finagle my money out of him. Just as I got there, someone knocked on the door. A man's voice said it was room service. He brought in a bottle of wine and said it was compliments of the man who was with me in the bar. Naturally, I assumed Nikos sent it—you know, trying to butter me up. This guy opened the bottle, poured out a glass, and handed it to me. Then he put the bottle down on the desk and left. Being the wine lover I am, and in a bad mood anyway, I drank down the entire glass."

"What kind of wine was it?"

"I'm not sure. The label was obscured. It was a deep burgundy color, a little bitter, but still tasty. Right after I drank it, I felt tired. I'm usually not after only one drink, so I thought that was kind of odd. When I couldn't keep my eyes open a moment longer, I must've dropped down on the bed. That's all I remember."

Heather gazed out the window, trying to recall what was in her aunt's room. "I didn't see a wine bottle or glass on the desk this morning. So whoever killed Nikos must have taken them to get rid of the evidence that you'd been drugged. Maybe he was drugged too, before he was shot." A quick and disturbing thought worried her. "Where's your gun?"

Julia turned her face away from Heather's gaze. "Yeah, well, that's another thing. It's gone. I checked my purse, but it wasn't there."

"Do you think it was *your* gun that was used to kill Nikos?"

Julia tilted her head. "Are you kidding me?" She grabbed Heather's hand. "Come on. Let's get out of here before housekeeping finds him."

Chapter 6

HEATHER stood firm. "I'll make coffee, and we'll think this over."

"Uh. No. Forget it. Have you tasted the coffee in our rooms? It's dreadful. So, let's stop wasting time and get out before it's too late. We can stop at Starbucks on our way out of town."

"You can't just run away. We have to call the police and get this whole thing straightened out."

"I can't get involved with the police. I've got warrants."

"For what?"

"Parking violations and traffic tickets."

"How many could you possibly have?"

"Seventeen. Maybe more. It came to a point where I stopped counting."

Heather's fingers tensed. "Why didn't you just pay them?"

"I never had the money or the time or the patience to go to court. Too much of a nuisance."

Aunt Julia's life really was a mess. "Is there anything else you haven't told me?"

Julia hesitated. Heather didn't like the guilty look in her eyes. Her aunt was definitely hiding something.

"Maybe I should hire a lawyer," Julia suggested.

"With what? You don't have any money, and besides, don't you think it would look a little suspicious to the police if you hired a lawyer before you even called them?"

Julia's eyes narrowed, and she ran a finger across her lips as if she was considering what to do. "Well, we can't just leave Nikos's body in my bed. That would look even more suspicious. Let's move him. If he's not there, no one will suspect me. They'll think someone else did it."

"That's completely insane! It would make us accessories after the fact. We'd get arrested. And anyway, his DNA is all over your room. Of course they're going to come looking for you."

Julia added a slight smile of defiance. "Who's gonna find out it was us who moved him? If anyone asks, just say you don't know anything. Deny. Deny. Deny. That's always been my philosophy."

Trying to trick the police was a bad idea. Even though her aunt probably didn't kill Nikos, taking the body out of her room would not only make her look guilty, it would mess up the crime scene and any evidence that might exonerate her.

Julia stomped toward the door. "If you're not going to help me, I'll do it myself!"

Heather put a hand on her aunt's shoulder to stop her. "Let's just call the police."

"You call. I'm leaving." Julia grabbed the door handle. "I only need an hour's head start."

"Where're you going? You can't hide. The authorities will find you."

A shadow of annoyance crossed Julia's face. "I got mob connections in Chicago. They'll know where to hide me where I'll never be found."

Her aunt was always a little eccentric, but this was downright crazy. "What connections?"

"Didn't your mom ever tell you your grandfather's uncle was Chicken Harry? He used to be Al Capone's bodyguard."

"I'm pretty sure I would have remembered if she had."

"My sister never could face the truth."

"Even if that's true, how is the mob going to help you?"

"The usual way."

Heather couldn't believe what she was hearing. "What *usual* way?"

Julia's eyes shifted from side to side. "I'm not sure. They'll come up with something. And I'll find them. I'm very resourceful. I've had to be."

Heather took a firm hold of her aunt's arm. "Stop talking like that. You're not going to find any mafia members. I'm calling the police." She picked up the phone.

Julia gasped. "If you're gonna do that, don't call from the phone in your room or your cell. Use a public phone. I think I saw one in the lobby. And make it anonymous."

"What's the difference? Honestly, Aunt Julia, you've been watching too many old noir movies."

Heather's stomach grumbled, partly from nerves and partly from hunger. On the way downstairs, she made a call to the local police from her cell and followed Julia to the small room off the lobby where a continental breakfast was set up. After pouring herself coffee, she added some milk and grabbed a croissant. Julia had coffee, black. They sat at a table in the corner as far away from the others as possible.

"Is the gun registered to you?" Heather whispered.

"No." Julia's usually ruddy face was now pale. "It's registered to Stan. If he says I have it, I'll insist I lost it."

"You have to tell the police the truth, or it will only make you look guilty. Just tell them your gun was missing when you woke up."

"I could say that." Julia rubbed her forehead.

"Are you sure you've told me everything?"

"Well, there's one little thing—"

Terrified screams cut Julia off A hotel maid ran into the lobby and stopped at the registration desk. "There's a dead man upstairs! Call the police."

Heather slapped a hand to her forehead. She'd neglected to tell the desk clerk about him. "I was hoping the police would get here before housekeeping found Nikos. Didn't you put the *Do Not Disturb* sign on your door?"

"Too late now." Julia sighed out a long breath. "I told you we should have left."

Heather jumped up, leaving most of her croissant and coffee on the table, and made her way to the front desk.

The well-dressed, middle-aged clerk had a phone to her ear. Heather waved at her as she read the name tag. "Um, Christine. I've already called the police. They should be here soon."

Christine glanced from side to side as she kept the phone where it was. "I'll call anyway, just to make sure."

Heather stood next to her aunt in the lobby and counted her heartbeats while she waited for the police to arrive, which wasn't hard since they were pounding against her chest.

Julia crept to the door and periodically glanced up and down the street. She pushed it open as if she was going to make a run for it, just as several squad cars and an ambulance pulled up in front of the hotel, blocking the entrance.

"Where do you think you're going?" Heather asked.

"I gotta get outta here." Julia clutched at her chest. "I need air." She grabbed a package of small mints from her pants pocket and popped one into her mouth.

A tall, husky police officer made his way to the door. "Are you ladies leaving?"

"No," Heather answered. "My aunt was just getting some air."

"You'll have to go back inside. There's been a homicide at this hotel, and we need to speak to everyone who was staying here this weekend."

Heather gave him a sickly smile. "I know. I'm one of the people who called you. The murder took place in my aunt's room." She breathed deep to calm her turbulent stomach and walked Julia back into the lobby, followed by two officers.

It didn't take long for the hotel lobby to swarm with police. Sitting down in the leather chairs, they watched an officer question the desk clerk.

Outside, the tall officer stationed himself at the door, and another was marshaled at the front desk, while two others accompanied the clerk and the maid into the elevator.

"Well, we almost made it," Julia whispered.

Heather chewed her thumbnail—something she hadn't done since grammar school. "I've never been so nervous."

Julia offered her a mint. Heather took it and popped it in her mouth. Anything was better than biting her nails.

The small crowd of people from the breakfast area had now gathered around the registration desk, their murmurs growing louder by the minute. It didn't take long before two officers appeared in the lobby again, followed by Christine, the desk clerk.

"May I have your attention," one officer announced. "There's been a homicide. So we need to take names and addresses. Please have your ID ready as we come to you."

The officer at the door let in a woman and two men, carrying bags and equipment. They headed straight to the elevator.

Julia's head bobbed up and down as she eyed them. "I've watched enough cop shows on TV to know that's probably the forensics team."

Heather caught her breath. "We forgot about fingerprints."

"Do you have any idea how many fingerprints there are in a hotel room? They might pull some prints that aren't ours from the door handle, unless the killer wiped it clean."

A short, robust-looking man in a black suit walked in and spoke with the officers. He approached the desk clerk. "Is there an empty room I can use for interviews?"

Christine directed him to a meeting room near the lobby.

After all the desk clerks and the housekeeping staff were called in and questioned, Julia was next. She popped another mint into her mouth and said, "Wish me luck."

***

When Julia finally walked out, fifteen minutes later, she looked a little wilted, but her natural cheerfulness seemed undaunted by the interview.

Officer Hendricks called Heather's name. Although she tried to keep the thought out of her mind, she was afraid they would arrest her aunt. She walked into the interview room to find the detective, white shirt, collar open, his thinning brown hair damp with perspiration.

A young police officer directed her to sit in the chair opposite him. "Miss Stanton, this is Detective Lindsey."

She greeted him, "Detective."

His dark eyes gazed at her face a moment, and he went right to the questioning. "Did you know the deceased, Nikos Stamos?"

"Only by sight. We were never formally introduced."

"Where were you between ten and midnight last night?"

"In my room, sleeping. No, actually I was watching an old mystery movie."

"What movie?"

Heather thought a moment. "One with an actor named, Errol Flynn, um... *Footsteps in the Dark,* I think."

He wrote something down, no doubt the name of the movie. "Did you hear any unusual noises or activity going on outside your door?"

"I know the walls are pretty thin here, but the television was on, so I doubt if I could hear what was going on in the hallway. If anything was… going on, I mean."

Skipping over what she said, he asked, "What's your relationship to Julia Fairchild?"

"She's my aunt."

"Since she admits to finding the body in her bed this morning, why did *you* call the police instead of her?"

"She was a little disoriented and couldn't think clearly, so I took charge of the situation."

"You mean, the two of you are in this together?"

Heather wasn't clear what he meant by that. It sounded like an accusation. "No!" Heat came up from deep inside, burning her face. "We weren't anywhere near each other when the crime was committed."

"You were seen in the lobby yesterday evening when Ms. Fairchild had an argument with the deceased in the hotel bar, and you followed her upstairs."

"I was in the lobby, but I didn't follow her. She walked up, and I took the elevator."

"Do you know what the argument in the bar was about?"

"I didn't last night."

"Yet you called after her."

"I did, because my aunt seemed upset." She probably shouldn't have said that. Too late now. "Aunt Julia didn't answer me. I saw her go up the stairs, and I returned to my room."

"And you didn't see her for the rest of the night?"

"No, I didn't."

He shoved his hands under his arms. "Did you see anyone in the hall on your way to your room?"

"No."

"Did you see your aunt this morning?"

"I did. She took me to her room to show me the... um, Nikos."

"Did you touch anything while you were in there with her?"

"I didn't touched a thing. She and I only talked."

"So you *do* know what was said last night. Why did you lie about it?"

"I didn't know what the argument was about last night until she told me about it this morning. I didn't lie about that part. Why are you trying to trick me?"

Leaning forward in his chair, he narrowed his eyes, his gaze severe. "Miss Stanton, why not look at this sensibly? I'm not your enemy. I'm only trying to track down the person who's guilty of murder and protect the innocent. I've got a hard job, and in helping shield a murderer, you're making that job even harder."

"Wait a minute," she said. "I'm not—"

He held up his hand. "No, *you* wait. I know you think you're doing the right thing, but look at it this way. If you're trying to protect someone you believe to be innocent, did it occur to you that you're helping the murderer cover his or her tracks while that other person remains under suspicion?"

"What makes you think I'm trying to protect anyone?" She realized too late a question like that was practically an admission.

He chose to ignore her slip for the moment. Proceeding with his own agenda, he continued to question her for the next ten minutes before he finally said," I understand you and your aunt were supposed to check out of the hotel this morning."

"That's right."

"May I suggest you check back in. I don't want either of you leaving town for a while. That's all for now. You can go." He motioned to the police officer. "Send in whoever's next."

With that abrupt end to their conversation, Heather left the room and met her aunt in the lobby. "Detective Lindsey said we need to check back in to the hotel. He doesn't want us leaving town just yet."

"He told me. I've already done that," Julia said. "They gave you the same room. Here's your new key card. I'm in the one next door." She sucked in a sharp breath. "The forensics team wants me to give them my clothes and shoes from last night. They're probably full of... you know... evidence. And they want to draw blood."

"Well, maybe there isn't anything on your clothes that could incriminate you. And the blood test should prove you were drugged. So that's good news."

"I don't know if it is or not." Julia shivered. "To tell you the truth, I'm afraid."

Heather put an arm around her aunt's shoulders. "Growing up, I always thought you were the bravest person I knew."

"Oh, sure," she admitted. "I may have looked brave, but I've always been a coward. It's funny that other people haven't seen it." There was silence for a few beats. "If I think I can't deal with something, I've always walked away. And I definitely don't think I can deal with *this*."

"You can't walk away forever. Things are bound to catch up with you sometime."

"Not if I play my cards right. Maybe there's a way —"

"Don't even think about it."

Julia hummed as if a fresh thought just came to mind. "Hey, Jack's a lawyer. Call him. Tell him to get down here right away. He can make this all go away."

Heather cringed. "It's useless to talk to Jack. He's not a criminal lawyer. He only handles divorce cases."

"A lawyer's a lawyer. They know how to do everything," Julia insisted.

Heather doubted that. She stared at her phone for a moment before choosing him from her contacts list. When she heard the deep timbre of his voice, anger rose up in her throat over the last time she called. Weakness in her knees forced her to sit down in a nearby chair. She wasn't ready to talk to him yet. Or possibly ever. Her hand trembled as she ended the call.

A moment later, the phone rang, Jack's name and photo lit up her screen. Heather never realized before how sharp her ring tone sounded. Now it pierced her eardrums. She let it ring.

Julia grabbed the cell from her hand and answered it. "Hello. No, this is her aunt, Julia Fairchild." She took the phone to the breakfast area for privacy. After a few minutes, she returned and handed the phone to Heather. "What good is a lawyer if he refuses to help? Here, he wants to talk to you."

Heather put the phone to her ear. "This has been a big mistake, Jack. There's nothing you can do. And there's nothing left for us to say to each other, except ... goodbye." She clicked off his call, and a sense of relief washed over her now that everything was over between them. Odd, she didn't regret it—not even for a second.

What she did regret was not leaving town right after dinner last night.

Chapter 7

A few police officers left with the forensic team after the coroner took the body away. Detective Lindsey remained behind, stubbornly determined to wear everyone down.

Heather traipsed back to her room and was followed in by her aunt. Julia sat in the chair and tapped her short nails on the desktop.

"What do you know about Nikos?" Heather asked.

"Not much."

"From the time you spent together, surely you must have found out something."

The long oval of Julia's face looked solemn, her small arched nose held high—her face tense in the effort to concentrate. "Let me think."

"What did you talk about?"

"Mostly horses, gambling. Our exes."

"Did he talk about any other relative besides his ex?"

"No."

"We're going to have to find someone who knows more about him." Heather tapped her chin, and stopped as a thought struck her. "Chad Willows."

"Who?" Julia asked."

"The guy who stopped at our table in the restaurant, yesterday."

Julia shook her head. "I don't trust him."

She must have had her reasons. Heather had no idea what to say or do to change her aunt's mind. The only thing she was certain about was that they could muddle through this nightmare with more confidence if someone from town was on their side. Chad had to know a lot of people since he grew up here. She pulled his card from her purse.

"Why don't you go back to your room and try to get some rest," she told her aunt. "I'm going to have a talk with him anyway."

"Why can't I stay if you're calling him?"

"I'm not calling. I'm going to the bookshop in town where he said he works. I'm a pretty good judge of character. When I see Chad in his own environment, I'll know if we can trust him or not. And if we can, I think this situation is better explained in person."

"I'll go with you."

Heather didn't need her aunt along to possibly blurt out the wrong thing, as she often did. "No, I'd better go alone."

As Heather walked out of the main lobby and into the bright sunlight, she almost ran into the police officer stationed there. "Am I allowed to leave the hotel?"

"As long as you tell me where you're going."

She pulled out the card Chad Willows had given her. "I thought I'd go to the bookstore in town and buy a novel to read. Can you give me directions?"

The officer glanced at the card, looked toward the street, and pointed. "Walk straight for two blocks and turn right for another block. It's on the corner. You can't miss it."

A young man holding a camera and a well-dressed woman jumped out of a white van with large letters on the logo. *Must be the local news station.* They caught up with her not far from the hotel, and the woman asked question after question about the murder.

Heather held her hands in front of her face. "Sorry, I don't know anything, I'm just a guest at the hotel. So, please go away. I have nothing to say."

They followed behind for a few steps, and eventually turned around.

***

The sign in the window of the two-story, red brick building said *New, Rare, and Vintage Books.* The wooden door with its oval etched glass told Heather it was very old. Inside, the tinkle of the bell hanging over the door surprised her. The cool air came as a refreshing relief from the hot sun beating down on her as she'd walked the three blocks to get here. *Oak paneled walls and wooden bookshelves. Impressive.*

She scurried past the hard covers and paperbacks to reach the back of the store and glanced around. When she didn't see Chad, she came back to the front.

"Can I help you?" a woman's voice asked.

She hadn't noticed the woman, and the unexpectedness of hearing the voice made her heart race. *Why am I so nervous?* Maybe this was a mistake. But now that she was here, she needed a reason. Without turning around, she said, "No, I'm just browsing."

Heather made her way to the mystery section and came across the Agatha Christie novels. She pulled out two paperbacks she hadn't read yet and strolled back to the front counter to pay.

There was a dark, magnetic beauty about the girl at the desk. Her thick eyelashes looked like jet against the pale color of her cheeks as she sat low behind the counter, reading one of the same books Heather had picked up. Could this be Chad's sister?

"So you're a Christie fan, too?" the young woman asked.

"My mom was a member of the Agatha Christie Society for many years. Guess I got my love of mysteries from her."

"So was my Grandfather." The clerk picked up a copy of *The Man in the Brown Suit.* "I've just finished reading this one. You're gonna love it." She scanned the book and said, "The cover's ripped." She pressed a button on the intercom attached to the wall behind her. "Would you get me another paperback copy of *The Man in the Brown Suit*? I've got a customer out here who needs a replacement." She proceeded to scan the other book, *Murder is Easy.*

A lithe, black feline jumped up on the counter. It looked up at Heather with large, inquisitive green eyes. She took a step back in surprise. Without blinking, the clerk lifted the cat up and set it back on the floor. "Don't mind Makkie. He's just nosy. He keeps the place free of field mice."

Heather was just about to ask if the clerk knew where Chad might be when footsteps approached and another copy of her book was tossed on the counter. She turned to see his smiling face looking down at her.

"Heather. I thought you were leaving town this morning."

"Actually, I was just about to ask your sister... um this *is* your sister, isn't it?"

Chad's eyes were full of humor as his lips curved into a warm smile. "Yes, this is my sister, Ashley. Ashley, this is Heather…"

"Stanton," she finished as the cat rubbed against her calf. Heather stooped down. "Hello, sweetheart."

The cat rushed away. She extended her hand, palm down, and he stealthily approached until he reached it, sniffed, and rubbed his face against her fingers.

"He likes you." Ashley sounded surprised. "You're lucky. He doesn't take to many people."

"My sister and I had a lot of pets growing up. At one time, we had two cats. I've always been an animal person." *Unlike some people.* Jack Steel's face flitted across her mind for an instant. She shook it off. "I'm sorry to say I don't have any now."

Heather stood and gazed into Chad's sky blue eyes. His look was so calming, it put her instantly at ease. She was sure she could trust him. "As I was saying, I was just about to ask your sister where to find you. I need your help. There's been an incident at the Franklin House hotel where my aunt and I are staying."

"I remember your aunt." Chad caught his sister's attention. "She looks a lot like cousin Gladys. Right down to the flaming, red hair."

Ashley's lips curved into a knowing smile.

Heather glanced from brother to sister. "I don't know if you've heard yet. Nikos Stamos was murdered in the hotel last night."

Chad's eyes widened. "Nikos was murdered?" His jaw tensed.

Ashley stared at Heather with her mouth gaping open. "A murder in this town? That's scary. This will definitely put a crimp in Benny's colon."

"Benny?" Heather asked.

"Detective Lindsey. He's got colitis."

"Sounds like you know him pretty well."

Ashley chuckled. "Cousin Gladys's ex-husband."

"Does Benny know who did it?" Chad asked.

Heather bit her lip. "He isn't saying. I think my aunt may be his number one suspect."

Chad let out a mild laugh. "Your aunt? Why would he suspect her?"

"It's a long story. Do either of you know a good criminal defense attorney?"

Ashley pointed to her brother.

"Oh no." Chad shook his head. "I'm through with all that. I'm just a book store owner now."

"You wouldn't actually have to defend my aunt. But we could use some advice. And since you knew Nikos —"

"Knew him?" Ashley interrupted. "Chad nearly married his daughter."

Her words tugged at Heather's heart. So that was why he cased the off-track betting place with such intensity yesterday. He was probably looking for her. "Is that so?"

Chad gave his sister a look that could have stopped a train. "She's exaggerating."

Ashley grinned. "Krystal Stamos said she'd never forgive my brother for breaking their engagement and leaving town two weeks before the wedding."

He clutched the collar of his shirt in a nervous gesture. "That was a long time ago. I'm sure she's gotten over it by now. Anyway, I hate to disappoint you. I'm not a lawyer. I once worked as a private investigator for a law firm."

"Well, that's okay too. At least you might be able to help. I don't have much money, but I'll be glad to pay you for your services."

With a stern look, Chad said, "I'm not in the PI business anymore."

If he didn't help, she'd have to swallow her pride and call Jack back, which was probably just what he was waiting for. She could envision the smug look on his face when he heard her voice again. It only made her more determined not to go to him for help. Not now or ever. Desperation brought a lump to her throat.

"Couldn't you make just one exception? If you can't help, at least tell me who can."

Ashley twisted a long strand of hair around her finger. "What's wrong with you, Chad? You're going to make this poor woman cry."

Chad took a deep breath and narrowed his eyes at his sister. He motioned toward the back of the bookstore. "We can talk back there."

"Wait for me." Ashley rolled her wheelchair out from behind the counter, Makkie the cat firmly in place on her lap. "I'm right behind you."

Seeing Ashley in a wheelchair brought back the memory of Derek telling Chad he was sorry about his sister's accident. She wanted to ask how it happened, but she didn't want to pry.

The bell over the door tinkled. Chad stopped and turned around. "You go to the front of the store and take care of that customer. I'll talk to you later."

He opened a door at the back of the store and put his hand out as an invitation for Heather to enter. She walked into the small, comfortable square room. An oak desk with a computer sat in the middle of the gray-tiled floor, and a black leather office chair was pushed under the desk.

Chad grabbed a tall pile of books from one of the folding chairs, set them on the floor, and pulled the chair up to the desk for her. Heather sat as she gathered her thoughts.

He took the seat in the chair opposite her. "Before you tell me anything, I have to inform you that I've let my investigator's license expire. I didn't renew it because I was leaving Chicago to come here to help my sister."

Heather's hopes sank. "Oh."

"Even though I'm not doing PI work anymore, I still may be able to help you and your colorful aunt, unofficially, of course."

"Colorful is a nice way of describing her. Nutty is a better description." She wasn't sure what he could do. As desperate as she was, she'd take all the help she could get right now.

Chapter 8

"TELL me why you think Detective Lindsey might arrest your aunt."

As she spoke, Chad leaned against the back of his chair and eyed her with curious interest. When she finished telling him what had happened, he let out a long, slow breath and rubbed his clean-shaven jaw.

"Do you have any idea where your aunt's gun might be?"

"No, and we're hoping they never find it."

"Do you know if your aunt fired that gun recently?"

"I couldn't tell you. Until yesterday, I hadn't seen her in over five years. I didn't know my aunt *owned* a gun, much less carried it around in her purse."

Chad stood. "Maybe I'd better have a talk with her."

He walked Heather back to the front of the store. From behind the counter, Ashley sipped a soft drink from a can as a tall and thin young man leaned over it and talked to her.

He straightened and turned toward them as they approached. "Hi, Chad."

"Kyle." Chad nodded to the young man and glanced at his sister. "We're leaving now."

Ashley raised her soda can. "Let me know how it turns out when you get back. Hey wait! Don't forget your books."

Heather paid and grabbed the books off the counter. The bell jingled again as Chad held the front door open for her.

"Is that your sister's boyfriend?" she asked as they walked toward the hotel.

"Kyle Edwards? It's hard to tell. He lives next door. He's had a crush on her since they were in grammar school. According to her, they're just good friends."

"He seems like a nice guy."

"He's okay. A computer geek. Not really my sister's type."

"What *is* her type?"

"She's always liked Derek."

Heather could understand that.

***

The same two news media people rushed up to them as they approached the hotel. The police officer fended them off and opened the door to the hotel lobby for Heather and Chad.

Chad gave the officer a quick nod of thanks, and proceeded to the front desk. "Hi, Christine. The media been bothering you?"

"Oh yes, but Detective Lindsey told everyone not to give out any information."

"Smart lady. So, where is Benny?"

"He's in room three twenty-five, where Nikos was killed. I moved Mrs. Fairchild to the room next to Miss Stanton."

They walked through the lobby and got into the elevator. At the third floor, Heather led Chad to her aunt's room and knocked on the door.

Julia opened it. "It's about time you got back. I've been sitting here watching the news about this God-awful murder on TV, and sweating like a pig. Thank goodness the police said they didn't have any suspects, and the body was found in one of the hotel rooms. Suppose I should be grateful to them for not naming names." Julia dabbed her face with a tissue. "Don't they have air-conditioning in this hotel?"

Chad walked over to the thermostat and set the dial on air-conditioning. "There. It'll be cooler in a few minutes."

Julia stared at the dial. "When you stay in these little hotels, nobody tells you anything. They expect you to know this stuff. Honestly, it makes me..." She gasped, and shook a finger at Chad. "Why were you following me around after I got off the train?" She took a few steps back. "What do you want from me?"

Chad put his hands up in a defensive gesture. "Honestly, it was a simple case of mistaken identity."

Julia folded her arms across her ample chest and tapped her foot on the floor. "That's a likely story."

"It's the truth," he said.

Heather couldn't believe how paranoid her aunt was. "Calm down, Aunt Julia. I believe Chad and I've told him everything about last night. He's here to help."

"Are you a lawyer?"

"No."

Julia waved him off. "Then you can't help."

Chad walked to the door as if he couldn't wait to get out of the room. "I'm going to talk to Benny."

"Benny?" Julia asked. "You mean that—pardon the expression—police detective?"

"Yeah."

Julia brought her fingers to her temples. "Mark my words. That man's out to get me."

"What makes you say that?"

"The looks he gave me during the interview."

"That's probably because you remind him of his ex-wife."

Julia trotted over to the mirror and admired her face while smoothing her hair in place. "Do you really think so?"

Chad exchanged glances with Heather. "I'm sure of it."

All Heather could do was watch him walk out the door. "You shouldn't be rude to Chad. He didn't have to come here."

Julia clasped her hands together. "I don't know what's wrong with me these days. I can't seem to control my tongue. I'm always lashing out at people—something to do with hormones. I'm at that age." She pulled a package of mints from her pants pocket and popped one in her mouth.

That was more than Heather wanted to know, but it explained a lot. "Can you take something for it?"

"I'd have to see a doctor to get my prescription refilled. So bear with me."

"I'll do better than that. We'll find a doctor together."

Heather grabbed her purse and one of her books. They walked out of the hotel room and directly into Chad and the police detective, having a discussion in the hall.

The detective eyed Julia. "Where are *you* going?"

"My aunt needs to see a doctor."

"Not feeling well?"

Julia narrowed her eyes and lifted her chin as she glared at him. "It's not something I care to discuss."

Heather had to stop herself from rolling her eyes. "Is there a doctor in town you can recommend, Chad?"

His lips curved into a sympathetic grin. "St. John's Hospital Care Station is two blocks west of here, across the street from the park." He checked his watch. "You'd better hurry. They close at two on Saturday. I recommend you go out the kitchen door, so you won't be bombarded with questions from those media people out front."

"Thanks. If we're not back in an hour or so, you'll know where to find us."

***

As they sat in the care station lobby, Julia tapped her pen on the clipboard she held. "I hate filling out forms. What am I supposed to put down as my address?"

"Just use the one you gave to your insurance company."

"Oh. Well, I don't live there anymore. And I can't give them my new address, because I don't live there either." Julia leaned back in her chair, her sorrowful-sounding sigh enhancing the dark circles under her eyes. "And I haven't exactly kept my insurance premiums up-to-date." She popped another mint.

Heather rubbed her thumbnail along her bottom lip, something she'd always done when making a tough decision. This was going to be an expensive doctor's visit, but there was no getting around it. And her aunt didn't need to be under more stress. She could sympathize. Now that she was no longer employed, her health coverage was gone too.

"Don't worry. Just fill out the forms and tell the clerk you'll pay with a credit card. I'll advance you the money. You can pay me back whenever."

"No, I can't let you do that."

"Don't be silly. Of course you can."

Julia perked up. "Well, if you insist. I wouldn't take it if I didn't know you had a lucrative job and could well afford it."

Heather's mouth opened and shut as she struggled against the urge to tell her aunt she'd quit. She *had* one of those jobs. All she had now was a small savings account to tide her over until she could get another. *I'd better start emailing resumes, or I'm gonna be in deep …*

Julia finished filling out the forms and handed them to the clerk.

Before Heather could finish the first page of her new book, Julia's name was called, and she disappeared behind the large swinging doors.

Heather tried to concentrate on the story as her phone vibrated continuously. She ignored the notifications as long as she could. Finally, she gave in, closed the book, and pulled the cell out of her pocket.

She hadn't checked her phone in a few hours. Some of the messages looked urgent—especially the one in all caps from her ex-boss. There were several from her former coworkers, and then there were the ones from Jack. She'd have to talk to some of these people eventually, especially her sister. Now was as good a time as any. It would probably be at least fifteen minutes before her aunt came back out.

She took a deep breath and let it out in one big whoosh, an attempt to release the dread in her heart. It didn't work. So she gathered up what fortitude she had left, glanced at the messages again, and chose the person who would be the most understanding and sympathetic. Emily was her first call. She'd have to update her on the latest concerning their aunt, anyway.

***

Julia came back into the waiting room with a grin on her face. She waved to Heather and headed toward the door.

Heather gathered her things and caught up to her. "You look happy."

"I am. I met a wonderful doctor, and his nurse is calling my prescription in to the pharmacy next door. I was talking to her about the murder, you know, casually asking if she knew anything about the deceased, as if I didn't. She told me Nikos has a daughter, Krystal. She's a model."

That figures. "Chad's sister mentioned her when I was at the bookstore earlier. I suppose she's one of those bone-thin fashion models."

"Underwear and swim suit."

Of course she is.

"You could've been a model yourself."

"I don't think so. For one thing, I'm only five-four, and for another..." Heather patted the bottom of her jeans. "I've got a little too much junk in my trunk."

Julia glanced at her niece's backside. "You're crazy. You look slim to me."

"Thanks." Heather wanted to believe her, but the mirror didn't lie. "Let's go pick up your prescription."

After they walked out the door, the click of a lock told Heather the clinic was closed for the day. "It's a good thing the drug store's next door." She took a few steps toward it, but Julia put a hand on her shoulder to stop her.

"Wait." She motioned toward the parking lot. "Do you see that tall, blond guy leaning against the lamp post, talking on his cell?"

Heather glanced in his direction. "Yeah. That's Chad's friend, Derek."

"You know him?"

"Met him once."

"He was the bartender at the off-track betting joint when I was in there with Nikos last night. What a hunk, and that smile. Made my knees weak."

She new exactly what her aunt meant. "Really Aunt Julia, you're old enough to be his mom."

"Killjoy."

Let's get your prescription."

"I can pick up that prescription anytime. Let's follow him for a while, just to see where he's going."

"We can't. We'll look like a couple of stalkers. And besides, we don't know this town. We might get lost."

Julia flung her arms upward. "Oh, for goodness sake. When did you lose your sense of adventure? Come on, it'll be fun."

Chapter 9

"STOP looking so tense," Julia said. "We just happen to be walking in the same direction as this guy. If he goes into some building, we'll take note of it and pass by."

Heather checked the time on her cell phone. "It's two-thirty. The police are going to come looking for us if we don't get back to the hotel."

Julia's eyes narrowed as her intense gaze followed Derek. She nudged Heather with her elbow. "Stop! He's going into that Chinese restaurant. Good, I'm starving. I only had coffee for breakfast, and with everything that's happened, we didn't have lunch. Let's go in."

Before Heather could say a word, Julia pulled the door open. She followed her inside just as Derek met up with a leggy brunette in a short navy dress that clung fashionably to her seductive figure. A white, silk scarf tied to a cobalt Prada bag hung on her shoulder. Long, straight hair was swept away from her face in an eighty-dollar blowout. The type that used to be in Heather's budget.

As she passed them, the scent of perfume lingered in

the air. It smelled of exotic flowers—expensive. Possibly French.

Since the lunch rush had passed, Heather and her aunt were seated right away. Both ordered egg rolls and shrimp in lobster sauce. Julia's eyes drifted back to the couple who were seated a few booths away.

"I wonder who she is. His lover?" Julia raised an eyebrow. "Maybe they did this murder together."

Heather was tempted to glance at their table. She restrained herself. "Don't go jumping to conclusions. You don't know these people. And speaking of murder, Detective Lindsey thinks we're coming right back to the hotel. I'd better call." Heather picked up her phone and stared at the screen. "I didn't get his number. Do you have his card?"

Julia dug in her purse and pulled it out. "Here it is. Before you do that, check out those two men who just walked in."

Heather moved her gaze to the door, but she couldn't see beyond the waiter who was bringing their tea. He set two cups and a teapot on the table and walked away.

"I don't see anyone."

"They hot-footed it to the pickup counter. That's okay. I took snapshots with my phone."

"Why?"

Julia lifted the teapot and poured some oolong into each of their cups. "Because they were at the OTB place when I was there with the dear departed. I got the feeling they weren't comfortable in each other's company."

Heather took a sip of tea. "What do you mean, not comfortable?"

"Well, kind of suspicious, as if something was going on among the three of them. Or at least between two of them. Maybe *they* killed Nikos. We really need to find out more about these guys."

The waiter set a plate of eggrolls on their table. Heather was never so glad to see food in her life. Based on the sly look in Julia's eyes, Heather would probably have to stop her from doing something reckless.

***

Julia shoved the last bit of food from her plate into her mouth and wiped her lips with a napkin. "The only thing I don't like about Chinese food is that after eating all this, I'll be hungry again in an hour." She slumped in her chair as if she was trying to avoid someone. "Don't look now, but that guy just walked in. It's a good thing we're finished eating so you won't be tempted to ask him to join us."

Heather's gaze drifted to the entrance as a stream of customers came inside. Chad stood at the front of the restaurant, glancing around. When he met Heather's gaze, he made his way toward them.

Heather acknowledged him with a gentle smile. "You didn't have to come and collect us. We're perfectly capable of getting back to the hotel on our own."

"Actually, I was just stopping in to pick up my lunch order when I saw you." He slid into the seat across from Heather. "While I'm here, I thought you'd like to hear about something I learned from Benny."

Julia crossed her arms as the waiter put their bill on the table. "Better be good news."

I hope Aunt Julia's prescription is magic that will transform her into someone who's pleasant to be around. "It's kind of you to stop by and give us any information you have."

He didn't answer as he stared past her at someone two tables away. The brunette with the long hair stood and turned to walk down the aisle. There was something languorous and passionate about the way she moved, as if she was strolling down a catwalk. And from the smug look on her face, she was wholly aware of its appeal.

Chad watched the tall, slender figure as she wandered toward them and stopped at their table. Her large coffee-colored, professionally made-up, eyes looked down at him.

"Hi," she breathed.

Chad frowned. "Sorry to hear about your dad. You have my sincere condolences."

Tears glazed her eyes. "Thanks. I flew in from New York as soon as I heard. He was such a great guy. I can't imagine why anyone would want to hurt him."

Julia jumped out of her seat. Heather grabbed her aunt's arm before she could utter a reproachful word and pulled her back down. "What my aunt wants to say is that we're so sorry for your loss."

The woman's nose scrunched as if she'd sniffed trash. "Who *are* you?"

"Oh, Sorry." Chad said. "These are my friends. This is Heather Stanton and her aunt, Julia Fairchild."

The woman's dark eyes moved from one to the other. A quick, fleeting smile crossed her gleaming, ruby lips before they plunged into a frown. "Krystal Stamos. Pleased to meet you."

Derek arrived at the table a moment later. He waved. "Hi, everyone. Just like the old days. Isn't it, Chad? The three of us together again."

Chad's face showed no emotion. "I think the past would be best forgotten."

Krystal let out a low sigh as she batted her long lashes at him. "Maybe some people aren't so easy to forget."

She turned on her silver sandals and strolled out the door on Derek's arm.

Julia leaned toward Heather's ear and cupped her hand over her mouth. "Somebody's carrying a torch."

Heather shrunk back in her seat. *That's obvious.*

Julia let out a low whistle. "So that's Nikos's daughter. Too bad she doesn't have a clue that her father was a no good, rotten—"

"Aunt Julia!"

Julia puffed out her cheeks. "Okay. Okay. Isn't she something? I can see *her* as an underwear model."

Heather straightened her slumped shoulders and tried to suck in the extra pounds she'd put on in the last year. So she didn't have a model's figure anymore. In the real world, very few women did. Anyway, she wasn't going to let it bother her. She had more important things to think about.

"What did you come here to tell us?" she asked Chad.

He stared at her as if coming out of his memories of the past. "Oh yeah. I um... I found out that Nikos was definitely shot in your aunt's bed sometime between midnight and two in the morning. Everyone in the hotel has been questioned, and no one heard a gunshot, probably because her room was at the end of the hall and there were no guests in the room on the other side. The police found a couch pillow that was used as a silencer."

Drawing herself up in her seat, Julia glared at him. "If they'd have tested my hands for gunshot residue this morning, they wouldn't have found any."

"According to the police, gunshot residue disappears pretty quickly, so no sense testing after eight hours. They're still searching for the gun and hoping your fingerprints will be the only ones on it."

"Well, of course my fingerprints will be on it." Julia opened her purse, pulled out a wallet, and checked inside. She looked up. "Unless someone wiped it clean."

"But you're still a suspect." Chad put his hand up before Julia could challenge him. "Let me tell you how I see things." He took his hand down. "There are two ways to look at this murder. Someone is trying to frame you, someone you know, possibly from your past who wants to get even with you for something you've done to them or to someone they love."

Julia drummed her fingers on the table. "At the moment, I can't think of anything I've done to anyone that would make them want to..." Her eyes moved in a wide, thoughtful arc. "Well, maybe. No, of course not. How would anyone know where I am?"

"Has someone threatened you?" Chad asked.

Julia's eyes scrunched. "Define threaten."

That didn't sound good. Heather would have to have a heart-to-heart with her later to find out more about who she suspected. "Let's not go there right now." She glanced around. A small group of people ate their meal in silence at the next table, and another was being seated behind them.

"This isn't the best place to talk about that. So, give us a quick version of the other way you see it."

Chad leaned toward them and brought his voice down. "Someone wanted Nikos dead, and your aunt was a convenient scapegoat. Maybe he knew something bad about someone and threatened to make the secret public, or he was blackmailing a person who couldn't afford to be blackmailed any longer."

Heather grabbed Julia's phone and did a quick search. She showed the screen to Chad. "Do you know these two men?"

"The short, scrawny guy is Johnny Tanner, Nikos's bookkeeper, and the tall, muscular one is Charlie Brasco, a former wrestler and local body builder. Goes by the nickname of Dutch. He runs the day spa and rehab center in town where my sister goes for treatment. Why do you want to know about them?"

Julia plunged her hand in her purse and pulled out a pen and a small notebook. "They look dicey." She wrote something down. No doubt the information Chad had just given. She stood and motioned toward the door with her head. "We have to go."

Chad slipped out of his seat. "If you'll wait a minute while I pick up my order, I'll be glad to drive you back to your hotel."

"No thanks," Julia insisted. "It's a beautiful day. We can walk."

While the outside temperature *was* near eighty, under a cloudless blue sky, this sounded like Julia wanted to do more than just walk.

Chapter 10

"We should find out where that spa is," Julia said as they walked toward the hotel. "I could use a massage. My muscles are so tense, I feel like a sardine that's been squished into one of those tiny cans."

"You can't afford a massage right now."

"I can't afford not to have one. You know how folks in small towns love to talk. I might be able to find out more about this guy, Dutch, and his dealings with Nikos. Besides, I've always been a sucker for wrestlers. Don't you remember all those Saturday nights your mom and I used to sit in front of the TV and watch professional wrestling?"

"How could I forget?" It started a few months after her dad, having a mid-life crisis, had run off with his young assistant.

Julia winked. "We weren't watching it for the sport, if you get my drift."

Sometimes her aunt's reasoning evaded Heather. "This isn't the time to be thinking about men."

"It's always the time for single women to think about men. This guy, Dutch, has got to be in his early fifties. I can tell by the gray in his hair, which is just about the right age for me, give or take a few. And that reminds me, I'd better pick up my prescription. And while I'm there, I'll need to get some hair color." She pulled a compact out of her purse and checked her hair in the mirror. "Can't expect to attract a man with *these* roots."

"You can't be serious."

Julia steered her toward the drugstore on the corner. "Never more serious in my life."

***

As they stepped out of the drugstore, Julia tramped across the street.

"You're going in the wrong direction." Heather grabbed her arm. "The hotel's this way."

"No, I want to go this other way toward the seedier part of town."

Heather couldn't imagine why. Her aunt must have had her reasons, so she tagged along just to make sure Julia didn't get into trouble. After walking a couple of blocks, the stores they passed advertised cheap goods, and the storefronts were grimy-looking. Some had broken and boarded-up windows.

A couple doors from the Salvation Army drop-off facility, Julia stopped. The store with a large display window covered in steel bars, displayed a dazzling array of merchandise from musical instruments to glittering gold watches and diamond jewelry. The orange neon sign flashed *Open*.

Julia smirked. "This is what I'm looking for."

"A pawn shop?"

"Where there's off-track betting, there's usually one of these. Gamblers tend to be desperate creatures when it comes to money. And I've always found it's a great place to get some ready cash."

"I can give you some cash if you really need it."

"No, no, no. I can't keep taking money from you. I've already taken enough."

"What are you going to pawn?"

Julia hesitated a moment. "I didn't really bring a lot with me. Most of my belongings are in storage in Chicago. I do have a few pieces of jewelry I've gotten as gifts I can part with. I hardly wear them anyway. And the nice thing about a pawn shop is that I can always get them back as long as I have my ticket."

***

Fifteen minutes later, they walked into the hotel lobby. At the front desk, Christine stood behind another clerk who was typing on a computer keyboard as she watched.

As Heather and Julia made their way to the elevator, Christine motioned for them to come over to the desk. "Hi." She checked the computer screen. "I just wanted to let you know that last night's stay was paid for by the railroad, but when I booked you two back into the hotel this morning, Julia Fairchild used her credit card, and it was rejected. So, I called the credit card company just to make sure there wasn't a mistake. When I finally got through, they told me to tell you to cut it up. Do you have another card you can use?"

Heather grazed her aunt with a look that said, "Is there anything else you haven't told me?" Julia dropped her gaze to the floor as Heather handed her credit card to Christine.

She inspected the card. "You can save some money if you share a room. Would you like to do that?"

Heather glanced at her aunt. "I suppose so."

Julia's right shoulder rose and fell as she gripped the drugstore bag tighter. She popped another mint in her mouth.

"In the morning, we can move both of you into the room next to the one you have now. Otherwise you'd have to pay for three rooms."

"That's fine," Julia said.

"Just stop by the desk to get your new key cards in the morning."

"Thanks," Heather said. They made their way to the elevator in silence. The door opened, and Detective Lindsey walked out. He and Julia stared daggers at each other as they passed.

The detective loosened his tie. "Got your medication, I see."

Julia stepped into the elevator and spun around to face forward. "Yes. Not that it's any of your business." Heather followed her in without saying a word—tired of defending her aunt's behavior. She'd forgotten just how trying Julia could be.

"When it's a murder investigation, *everything* is my business," he said just as the doors closed.

Riding up, Heather didn't know where to start the conversation. She didn't want to hurt her aunt's feelings, but things were getting out of hand. She opened her mouth to ask what Julia was going to do about her credit card, when Julia said, "I think I'll use the money I get for my jewelry to make a payment on my card and get a facial." Julia rubbed her cheek. "I really need one."

Stepping out of the elevator, they each darted back to their own rooms. Heather threw some clothes in her suitcase, to get ready for her move to the other room in the morning, when someone knocked on her door. She peered through the peephole. Julia's eyes stared back at her.

Heather opened the door, and her aunt flew in. "I just wanted to let you know I'm leaving for the pawn shop now. Got to get there before they close. While I'm there, I'll call the spa and see when they've got an opening."

"Wait." Heather grabbed her purse. "You're not going anywhere in this town alone. Especially if someone is out to frame you for murder. I'm going with you."

"If you insist. But I assure you, no one knows where I am, so I don't think I'm being framed. Now we have to look for who had a motive to murder Nikos, besides me." Julia turned and sprinted out the door.

Heather followed.

Julia power-walked as if she was on a mission. Heather checked the time on her cell. The store wouldn't close for another half hour. "You don't have to run. We'll make it."

Puffing now, Julia stopped to catch her breath. "I'm not taking any chances. You don't know the proprietors of the stores in these small towns. They open and close whenever the whim hits them."

It wasn't long before they made it to the pawn shop. Julia, whose face was now bright red and dripping with sweat, grabbed the door handle.

Heather backed up a few steps.

Julia turned. "Aren't you coming inside?"

"No." Heather bent over and inhaled a deep breath as she waited for her heartbeat to slow. "You go in. I'll wait for you out here.."

Julia wiped her face with a tissue. "Suit yourself."

As she waited, Heather paced in front of the store and let the warm afternoon breeze dry the perspiration from her face. She hadn't power-walked in a long time. It was something she'd done nearly every day for years, before she met Jack. Then the exercise stopped. He'd taken up all her spare time with events he needed to attend or things he wanted to do. She remembered reading about how falling in love makes you gain weight. And she had. Too many late night dinners out. Now that she was out of love, it shouldn't take long to lose it again. Today would be a good start.

A sleek, black, late model Lexus drove past her at a snail's pace. She reached into her purse and placed a hand on her pepper spray as she glanced inside to see who was driving. Chad waved. She waved back. *Did he decide to eat his lunch at the restaurant? If he did, this seems an odd route for him to take home. He said he lives across the park, several blocks in the opposite direction.*

Julia walked out the door of the shop with less than a self-satisfied grin on her face. She popped a mint.

"What's wrong?"

"I didn't realize how little my jewelry was worth. Men! You can never trust them. You think they're buying you the expensive stuff." She munched on the candy. "Those cheapskates."

"Sorry you didn't get what you thought you would."

"I'll just have to make the most of what I did get." She flashed a business card in front of Heather's eyes. "While I was in the shop, the guy behind the counter gave me the number of the spa. I called, and as luck would have it, they had an opening this afternoon. So, I'm in."

"Do you really want to spend your money on a massage?"

Julia stared at her, eyes wide. "Not just a massage. A massage, a facial, and a chance to get loads of information on a man who could be the murderer. You're right, I can't afford it." She frowned, and her shoulders drooped as she sauntered a few steps down the sidewalk alongside Heather. "But you can." Her voice had a renewed enthusiasm. "I'll just tell them I made the appointment for *you*."

"Me?" *I can't afford this either.*

Julia put a hand on her niece's shoulder. "You need to relax. You should see your face. If you keep your muscles tense like that, the lines will become permanent. It's not a flattering look."

Heather unclenched her jaw and relaxed her cheek muscles and her forehead. This wasn't the first time someone had said the same thing about her face in the past few months. It started around the beginning of her burn out. Tense was a look that had become a bad habit. Her aunt had a valid point. She did need to relax. She'd start with a short massage and follow it with a tall Tom Collins.

"And besides..." Julia batted her short lashes at Heather in an, *I'm innocent* look. "You don't want to see your poor old aunt convicted of a crime she didn't commit, do you?"

"Of course not, but I don't know the first thing about investigating murder. My specialty is writing ad campaigns."

Julia stood in front of her, feet firmly planted on the ground, arms folded across her multi-colored blouse. "And how's that working for you?"

Not well at all. Maybe it's time I tried something different. "All right. I'll do it." Just like her mom, Julia knew exactly how to push her buttons to get a reaction. "Where's the spa?"

Chapter 11

THE masseuse's gentle, firm hands worked their magic on Heather's neck and shoulders. She closed her eyes and gave in to the relaxing effect. She'd opted for the quickest and cheapest massage the spa offered. Fifteen minutes for thirty dollars. She'd never been comfortable with a stranger's hands on her, but this was heaven.

Julia had insisted on getting the facial so they could each question different employees at the same time. Between the two of them, they might find out something useful about this guy, Dutch. It was time to get a conversation started. She'd kept quiet, not wanting to get too friendly too soon or sound like she was being nosy.

"That feels great," Heather finally said. "Have you been doing this long, umm...? *What was the name on her tag again, Karen?*

The woman kept her hands working the muscles on Heather's back. "Oh, I've been doing this for more years than I care to admit."

"Well, you certainly know your job."

"Thanks. I also do facials, answer the phone, and relieve at the front desk."

"Have you been working here long?"

"Since we opened, ten years ago."

"Mind if I ask how you got this job?"

The masseuse lifted her hands from Heather's back. "Why? Are you thinking of applying for a position?"

"I might, if there's an opening. I'm currently between jobs." Not that she was qualified to do anything here.

"We're done."

The masseuse handed her a spa towel and grabbed one to wipe her own hands. "I don't think there are any openings right now. You'd have to check with Dutch."

"Is he the owner?"

"Part owner. He's also the manager." She motioned toward the wall with her thumb. "He's working out next door at the fitness center right now, if you want to talk to him."

"He's only part owner?"

"You must be new in town with all these questions."

"I just arrived yesterday."

"Nikos Stamos is, well *was*, his partner." The masseuse crossed her arms. "If you think you can get past Dutch by going directly to Nikos for a job, you're mistaken. He's..." She sucked in a deep breath as her gaze dropped to the floor. "Dead now. Murdered last night. Rest his soul." She sniffled and wiped a tear from the corner of her eye with her fingertips. Horrible, just horrible."

This is an interesting twist. Heather put a hand over her mouth in pretend surprise. "I'm sorry to hear that. Were you and Nikos close?"

Karen gazed around the room, as if she didn't know where to look. "We were at one time. Dutch is my boyfriend now."

"Nice guy?" Heather cringed at the lameness of her own question.

"The best."

Of course she'd say that about him. Quick, think of something else. "Has he been the manager long?" *Another lame question.*

"As long as I've been here." With her eyebrows scrunched in suspicion, Karen glanced up at the clock "If you'll excuse me, I'm meeting him for a drink in a few minutes." She must have thought that sounded like they were having cocktails, because she added, "In the juice bar at the fitness center. You should try their wheat grass smoothie sometime. It'll make you feel like a new woman."

"I'm sure it will. Thanks for the great massage. It was just what I needed."

Karen's thin lips curved into a small grin. "You're welcome. I hope you'll come again. And good luck finding work around here. Jobs are scarce." She gave Heather a sideways glance. "Honestly, you'd be better off going to some other town for a job."

That was kind of rude. Sounds like she's hanging on here for dear life.

After Karen left the room, Heather sat up and grabbed her blouse. *I hope she doesn't think I'm interested in her boyfriend.* If she'd learned anything in thirty-something years, it was never to question a girlfriend about the man she's dating. She couldn't wait to give this information to her aunt.

***

Heather walked out of the massage room as Chad Willows walked in the front, glass door.

"What are you doing here?" They asked simultaneously.

Heather smoothed the top of her hair. *I must look messy.* "I just came in for a quick massage. And you?"

"I'm picking up my sister. Ashley comes here to get her hair washed and blown out after she finishes therapy next door." Chad glanced up at the small enamel clock on the stark wall. "She's always the last customer on Saturday afternoon. How was it?"

"How was what?"

"The massage?"

"Oh. Relaxing. Just what I needed after a day like I've had."

"I can imagine. It was pretty rough, huh?"

"It was."

A buzzing noise came from the back of the room. Heather turned around as Ashley's motorized wheelchair rolled in and stopped next to her.

"Hi," she said. "How did everything go with your aunt? Was Chad able to help you?"

"Yes, he was very helpful."

"You ready to go?" Chad asked his sister.

"Uh huh."

Heather side-stepped the aisle so Ashley could pass. Chad's gaze returned to Heather. "If you're not doing anything tomorrow, would you and your aunt like to come to our house for a late lunch? We're having a few people over. I'm barbequing in the backyard. Just a casual get-together. Tomorrow should be very pleasant. I mean, weather-wise."

A free meal? "Thanks for the invitation. I'll have to check with my aunt, but I'm pretty sure we don't have any plans."

"I hope you'll come," Ashley said. "I'd really like to meet your aunt."

"Chad pulled out his business card and wrote their address and phone number on the back. "Give us a call if you can't make it. Drop in around one. Food will be on the table at two."

Heather took the card and smiled. "If my aunt agrees, we'll see you tomorrow. Can I bring anything?"

"If you want to bring something to complement the meal, I'm grilling steaks."

Chad opened the door for his sister. Heather watched them leave before walking to the counter to pay for her massage and Julia's facial. She was just about to sit in the lobby to wait, when her aunt stormed into the room. She stopped in front Heather and tapped her foot on the marble tile. "I hope you didn't pay for this, yet."

"Shhh," Heather whispered. "Why?"

"I doubt these people are professionals." Julia brought her voice down. "I'm sure the woman in there didn't know what she was doing. I've had a lot of facials. I don't know what *that* was except a complete waste of time and money."

Heather gazed at her aunt. "Your face looks..." *about the same.* "Very nice. But I take it you didn't learn anything about Dutch from her."

"I didn't say that." Julia glanced around. "Sometimes when people aren't good at what they do, they try to cover up their incompetence by talking. And this lady never shut up. Let's get out of here, and I'll tell you all about it."

On the walk back to the hotel, Heather told her aunt what she'd found out about Karen being Dutch's girlfriend and Nikos being his partner.

Julia listened and gave a terse nod. "I don't think I'll have a chance with Dutch, if he has a girlfriend. And it's just as well. From what I hear, he owed Nikos a bundle. I'm guessing gambling debts. Men who owe big bucks make me nervous." She shivered. "I learned that the Day Spa is hanging on by a thread. It hasn't operated in the black for over a year. Dutch might have to declare bankruptcy if Krystal decides she wants his half of the business to cover his debt."

That explains why the masseuse told me good luck finding a job here.

Julia was silent for a few moments. Her stoic expression left no hint as to what she was thinking. "And speaking of Krystal—"

"I didn't think we were."

Julia continued as if she hadn't heard Heather's remark. "Do you think she's going to reopen the off-track betting place for the Kentucky Derby next weekend? It might be to her advantage."

"You shouldn't be thinking about gambling right now. Not in the sad shape your finances are in."

"Horseracing isn't gambling. It's an art. If you know what you're doing, you won't risk that much, and if you don't know, you shouldn't be betting in the first place.

Anyway, sometimes you have to do the wrong thing at the right time to get what you need."

What does that *mean?* Heather shook off the feeling her aunt had plans she wasn't telling her about.

"I ran into Chad Willows and his sister at the spa earlier. They invited us to a barbecue at their house tomorrow afternoon. I told them I'd check with you."

"I still don't trust that man."

"What makes you say that?"

"He just happens to stop by the Chinese restaurant where we're having lunch to pick up an order and give us information. And now he's at the spa at the same time we are. Sounds just a little too coincidental to me."

Heather didn't mention that he'd driven past her on the street earlier. "I guess it does, but how would he know we were here?"

"Someone from the front desk could've called him. Listen... strangers don't just invite you to their house for a barbecue without an ulterior motive." Julia raised her eyebrows in a *you know what I mean* look. "I think he's up to something." She balled her hand into a fist and pushed it against her stomach. "I can feel it in my gut."

"Maybe you're being paranoid." *I know what you mean.*

Julia walked next to Heather in silence with her eyes scrunched. "I think we should go to that barbecue. For one thing, it doesn't look like there's much else to do in this town on a Sunday. And for another, I don't want to stay cooped up in that hotel room all day watching news, weather, and bad movies on television."

Heather couldn't have been more relieved. "I have to admit, it's a pretty dreary way to spend a Sunday. And I want to be convinced, one way or the other, that Chad can be trusted. While we're there, we might find out more about Dutch.

Julia tilted her chin up and smirked. "Now you're talkin' my language. Where's this guy's house, anyway?" Heather showed her the address, which Julia loaded into the street finder app on her phone. "This place is on the other side of town. We can't walk all that way. In this warm weather, we'll be drenched in sweat before we get there. Weren't you supposed to be renting a car?"

With everything that happened, Heather had forgotten. "I'll do it right now. I hope they're still open." Another expense she couldn't afford.

Chapter 12

On Sunday morning, Heather awoke to the weather report coming from the clock radio. The time, eight-thirty. She touched the off button.

A knock on the door startled her. She slipped out of bed and looked to see who it was. As soon as she opened the door, Julia bounced in. Although she'd muted her hair color to a bright auburn last night, the short-sleeved blouse she sported this morning was covered with flowers in riotous shades of reddish purple and scarlet, worn over a knee-length, crimson skirt.

Heather groaned. *Good grief!* "Why are you up so early?"

"It's Sunday. I gotta go to church."

Heather cleared her throat. "I know my mother goes to church on Sundays, but I never saw you go."

"I used to when I was young." Her eyelids lowered. "Well, I kinda promised God I'd start going again from now on if he'd lead me to Nikos's killer."

Heather rubbed her forehead. *Where does she get these ideas?* "Somehow, I don't think it works that way."

Her aunt sat on the edge of Heather's bed and slipped her feet into the pair of candy-apple red stilettos she carried. "How do you know? Have you ever tried it?"

"Can't say I have."

"Well, I'm not taking any chances." Julia grabbed her phone, touched the screen, and put it to her lips. "Churches in Willow's Bend, Illinois."

The voice on the phone answered, "Churches in Willow's Bend, Illinois. Sure."

Heather stood over Julia to see what the results were. Several photos showed up on the screen, along with addresses and other pertinent information.

Julia sprang to her feet. "Great, there's one around the corner and down the block." With a white cardigan over her arm and her purse in hand, she strolled toward the door.

"Just a minute! You're not going anywhere in this town without *me*."

"It's just around the corner."

"I don't care if it's just out the door. You're not going without me." Heather darted to the bathroom. "I'll be out in fifteen minutes. If we miss the first service, we can attend the next. You wait right here."

Julia slipped a lime green compact from her purse and applied a light coating of powder to her face. "I've taken care of myself pretty well up until now. I don't need you to hover over me."

Heather never showered so fast in her life. She towel dried and stuck her head out the bathroom door. "Are you still here?"

No answer.

Her towel slipped from her hand and dropped to the floor. "I knew it." She dialed Julia's cell phone. It went to voice mail. She threw her phone on the bed and picked up a yellow post-it note stuck to the pillow.

My dear niece,

I'll be okay. Don't worry. Be back in time for the barbecue.

You sit tight.

Auntie J.

Heather tore up the note. "Oh no! If anything happens to her, the family will blame me. I can hear them now: 'If you'd just been more conscientious. If you'd watched her more closely. If you'd been more careful ...'" Her eyes stung.

"I won't fall apart. I won't..." she repeated, but it was just like Friday afternoon in the office when she was blamed for things over which she had no control. Her enormous work load was more than her frayed nerves could handle. Stress overwhelmed her emotions, and she'd lost it completely in a vicious rant at her boss, which ended in her quitting.

Until then, she'd hardly ever lost her cool. Maybe her mother was right when she told her she shouldn't keep her feelings bottled up because she might explode. It had already happened once on Friday—actually twice. The second time when she found Jack with...

She pushed that thought out of her mind and focused on her inner calm, the way she remembered from the yoga classes she'd paid a fortune for but seldom attended. Closing her eyes, Heather took a deep, cleansing breath. *I refuse to let my emotions overwhelm me.* Or is it, *My emotions will never overwhelm me again?* Either way, the short mantras helped.

Why was she overreacting to Aunt Julia leaving? Her aunt could take care of herself. After all, she was just around the corner at church. What could happen to her there?

Just about anything. Heather didn't have to dig deep to ramp up some dogged determination to find her aunt. The responsibility for Julia leaving was all her own. She should have known better than to leave the woman alone.

Scooping the towel up from the floor, Heather made her way to the bathroom to get dressed. How hard could it be to spot a bright auburn-haired, middle-aged woman wearing a gaudy red outfit, in a church crowd? Willow's Bend was a small town.

***

Heather scanned the desk looking for her rental car keys. They weren't where she'd left them. She checked the drawers, the bed, the floor, her purse. No luck. *Don't panic. They have to be here somewhere.*

She retraced her steps from the night before. An awful thought crossed her mind. Julia must've taken them. Why would she need a car to go around the corner? Unless... She didn't even want to think about what her aunt might be doing this morning.

She'd have to go out to look for her on foot. Heather flipped off her heels and slipped into a pair of sandals. Waiting at the elevator, two hotel guests approached. Each lady eyed her, and when she looked at them, they turned their respective glances in another direction.

The young blonde wearing blue spandex and white running shoes said, "Excuse me. Aren't you related to the red-haired lady who found the dead body in her bed yesterday?"

Not knowing if she should admit it, but not wanting to be rude, Heather gave a quick nod.

The blonde tapped the older woman's shoulder. "See, Kate? I told you it was her."

Kate, a short brunette, also dressed as if she was going out for a run said, "You have our sympathy. It must have been a horrible ordeal for both of you."

"Yes," Heather admitted. "It was gruesome." The elevator dinged, and the doors opened. *Thank goodness*. They all stepped in.

On the quick ride down, the blonde said, "If you don't mind my asking, do you think she killed him?"

Heather spun around to face the lady, heat burning her cheeks. "Absolutely not!" When the elevator doors opened in the lobby, the two women left, whispering to each other as Heather made her way to the breakfast room.

I can't believe those two. Who asks that sort of question?

At the coffee station, Heather poured some in a to-go cup and clicked on the lid. She crossed the room to leave but couldn't resist the smell of bacon, eggs, and fresh bagels. Her stomach rumbled. She hadn't had a bagel in a long time. Jack never liked them.

Loud whispers had her glancing around. Stares from the people who crowded the tables followed her every move.

An elderly lady poked another sitting next to her. "That's the niece of the woman who found Nikos's body in her bed," she said. "Wonder where the aunt is?"

Heather didn't wait to hear any more. She grabbed a plain bagel, slapped some cream cheese on it, and wrapped the whole thing in a couple of napkins before she ran out the front door of the hotel.

***

Heather finished her breakfast, and downed the rest of her coffee as she approached the church—a large white, brick building with a tall steeple. Her rental, an Arctic-Blue Metallic Chevy Malibu, was parked in the lot. Instead of going in and disturbing the service to look for her aunt, she waited on the front steps.

Even though she had problems of her own, they seemed insignificant now in comparison with her aunt's. But helping Julia was also a way of helping herself get back on track after that embarrassing loss of self-control at the office. And the worse one when she got home. Now she could never return to her former office, or to the North Michigan Avenue condo she shared with Jack. Not that she wanted to.

A new start wouldn't be easy with no place to live, no prospects for a job that paid the kind of salary she was used to getting, and only the money left in her bank account.

Right now, her priority was to do everything in her power to keep her aunt from being arrested, which didn't look too promising at the moment. She tried to calm her troubled thoughts and put her problems behind her for the afternoon. It was Sunday, and there was a barbecue to attend in a few of hours. Her heart mellowed at the thought of being near Chad Willows again.

He couldn't be the sinister guy her aunt made him out to be. Not with the sweet way he was with his sister. He was almost too good to be true.

I think a little light Internet stalking may be in order.

She pulled out her phone and did a search on the public records database for Chad Willows living in Willow's Bend.

The results showed a Chadwick Emerson Willows, the third. *That must be him.* Two years older than her, he had one younger sister, Ashley, and one younger brother, Jamison.

Graduated from Loyola University, cum laude. *Impressive*

Heather's mom didn't have the money to send her to college, especially after her dad left, so she attended classes on weeknights and Saturdays, after working a full-time job during the day to pay most of the tuition herself.

No criminal record, but he did do ten days for contempt of court last year. Probably had to do with client confidentiality. *Have to admire a P.I. for that.*

Never married. He worked as a private investigator at Hurst, Rankin, and Steele. Heather sucked in a short, harsh gasp. "That's Jack's law firm!" Her hand, holding the phone, fell to her side. There was no need to read any further.

She paced the sidewalk thinking about what this meant. Then it dawned on her. *Oh, my God! Jack's having me followed.*

She dropped her shoulders and let out a long, agonizing breath. And just when she was beginning to like Chad. Even though the morning was warm, a cold chill ran through her. To think she almost fell for his charming good-looks and his seemingly good intentions. She should've looked him up sooner.

Heather located her car in the parking lot and stood in front of it, holding wild, imaginary conversations with Chad Willows in her head. After she'd exhausted every nasty sentence she could think of, an alternative came to mind. *I could call Jack and confront him. He'd probably tell me I was imagining it. He was a master at gas lighting.*

It might be better if she kept this information under wraps while she went along with their agenda. Maybe she'd drop a few hints to Chad that she knew he was following her, just to shake his confidence. When she wore him down and he admitted it, she'd tell him off with the full force of her anger.

Aunt Julia was right not to trust him. Of course, Heather would never admit that to her aunt. She never knew what Julia might blurt out. Or when.

Chapter 13

JULIA limped out of the church, grunting. She made her way toward the car and waved at Heather. "I'm so glad you came." She grabbed the car keys from her purse and handed them to her niece. "These shoes are killing my bunions. My feet are getting too wide to wear them. Do you want 'em?"

"No, I don't want your cast-off shoes." Heather took the keys and opened the car. She slipped in behind the steering wheel as Julia got into the passenger's side. As soon as her backside touched the seat, Julia flipped off the stilettos. "Whew! That's better."

"I told you not to go without me. Don't you realize how dangerous that could be? People in this town are starting to look at us as if you're guilty of Nikos's murder."

"So let 'em look. I just wanted to think things over. I know it's bad to speak ill of the dead, but that rat stole my money, and I needed a little quiet time to figure out how to get it back from whoever killed him and stole it." She crammed a small newspaper into her handbag. "Didn't you read the note I left?"

Heather started the engine and rolled down the windows to get some air in the hot car. "I did. Why did you take the car if you were only going around the corner?"

"Are you kidding? These shoes may look great, but I'd never have made it here if I had to walk."

Heather got into the queue of cars waiting to get out of the parking lot as her aunt shoved her purse to the floor board. She glanced at the newspaper sticking out of the top. The part of the headline she could read said, *Kentucky Derby*. So her aunt had gone out early to buy a racing form. Attending church was just an excuse.

When her rental finally got to the front of the queue, a black Lexus slowly passed in front of it with Chad driving and Krystal Stamos in the passenger's seat. *What are those two up to so early on a Sunday morning?*

Julia pulled a tube of bright red lipstick from her purse and applied a thick coat. "Hey, isn't that the guy from yesterday? What's his name, Chad something, and that underwear model?"

"Maybe they're going to church."

"Or maybe he's dropping her off after a night of debauchery."

Heather didn't doubt it. Why should she care what they were doing? "They can do what they like. It's none of my business."

"What do you mean? What if they were in on this murder together? I mean like... he did it, and she paid him?"

"Well, that's one scenario. It seems unlikely to me. Maybe we'll find out more at the barbecue this afternoon." She couldn't wait to see what secrets she could pry out of him. "Please, whatever you do, don't accuse anyone of anything until we find some evidence."

Julia fluttered her fingers in the air. "Don't worry about me. I'm the soul of discretion."

At the hotel, they each picked up their new key cards from the desk clerk

***

On the way to the Willowses' house, Heather stopped at a liquor store and bought a couple of bottles of Merlot. A question had been niggling at the back of her mind since she found out about Chad, so after she got back in the car, she asked her aunt, "When we were at the restaurant Friday evening, and you took your gun out after Chad had left our table, you said not to worry because he wouldn't be bothering us again. Why did you say that?"

"Well, I thought he was following me. And he's got that look." She raised a finger in the air.

"What look?"

Julia's eyes bugged out. "He looks like one of those confidence tricksters: clean-cut, all-American, and sneaky as a weasel."

Where does she come up with these ideas?

Julia's eyes narrowed. "I'm talking about men who appear to be trustworthy and likable. In reality, they're just out to get..." She shook the finger at Heather. "You know."

Heather was going to explain that Chad wasn't out to get anything from her because she didn't have much. He was just employed by Jack to follow her. But it was useless. Julia lived in her own little world.

Heather turned a corner and checked the GPS in the car. It said to take the next left to reach her destination. But the next left was a private drive leading to an enormous, historic-looking, three story house.

She glanced at her aunt. "This can't be the place."

Julia flipped the card Chad had given Heather over in her hand. "This is the correct street, and that's the house number on the card, so it must be right."

The house stood at the end of a short curving drive, its front veiled in the showering green foliage of two ancient weeping willows. She could only catch a hint of a high roof, a protruding balcony, and an aspiring turret. *I didn't think P.I. work paid this well.*

Heather turned in to the driveway and parked a few yards past the front windows. She got out of the car and rang the doorbell.

No answer.

She rang it again. Still no answer. Voices came from the back of the house. She motioned with her finger. "Maybe they're in the yard."

"Yeah." Julia sniffed the air. "I smell food cooking."

Heather flipped her mass of auburn hair over one shoulder and pushed her sunglasses to the top of her head as they followed the scent along a stone walkway. It led around the side of the house to an enormous cement patio area with an in-ground swimming pool behind it.

Chad stood in front of a huge silver gas grill, wearing a white chef's apron. He held a barbecue fork in his right hand with a raw porterhouse steak hoisted on the end of it.

Across from him, Derek, Chad's bartender friend, checked the bottles at a Kon-tiki style bar adjacent to the pool.

Julia nudged Heather with her elbow. "Wow! This is some joint, huh?"

Heather jerked out of a state of bemused wonderment. "Yeah, it's something, all right. Not quite what I was expecting." Judging from the ancient bookstore their grandfather had left them, she expected them to live in a modest little home. Tis was an estate.

Ashley moved her motorized wheel chair to the end of the patio and motioned for them to join her. "Hi! So glad you could make it."

Heather sauntered up to meet her and handed her the wine bottles.

Ashley accepted them. "Thanks. Merlot is my favorite." She turned and called out, "Hey, Chad, look who's here."

Chad set the steak on the grill and rushed over. "I'm happy you decided to come. It's great to see you again."

Heather couldn't bring herself to meet his gaze. She drew on every reserve to force a smile. "It was kind of you to invite us."

Julia gave an intense nod. "Nice place you've got here."

Ashley gazed up at her. "It's our family home." She handed the wine bottles to her brother and put a hand out. "You must be Heather's Aunt Julia. I'm Chad's sister, Ashley."

Julia shook hands as her eyes gave the back of the house a quick once-over. "So, tell me all about this family of yours."

Ashley steered her wheelchair toward the house, and Julia fell in step beside it. As they moved away, Heather was suddenly aware she was alone with Chad. She avoided his gaze. A middle-aged woman walking toward them, held a large bowl, and was followed by a short, middle-aged man with a slight paunch. They appeared to have come out of the bushes to her right.

The woman set the bowl down on the long picnic table. "I brought a salad."

Heather recognized the woman as Christine, from the hotel.

The man headed to the bar and selected a beer. He sat across from Derek on one of the tall stools. Heather's gaze followed the couple as they made themselves at home.

"That's Christine Talan," Chad said. "And her husband George is sitting at the bar. They live next door. Christine comes over to help Ashley whenever she needs it."

"What does her husband do?"

"George is an over-the-road truck driver, so he's gone for days at a time. Christine works at the hotel for a few hours, and she also takes classes at the local junior college, just to keep busy."

Ashley's friend, Kyle Edwards, came from behind them, holding a large plastic bag. "I brought more ice."

"Great!" Chad said "Just put it in the freezer by the bar."

George waved his arm. "Hey Chad, I think your steaks are burning."

"Excuse me." Chad held up a finger then turned and rushed away.

Heather made her way across the patio to sit at the bar.

"Would you like a glass of Chardonnay or would you prefer the Merlot?"

"I'll have the Merlot, thanks. Are you working today, or are you just a guest here?"

Derek leaned across the bar. "Bartending isn't really a profession for me. I'm actually the mayor's assistant. I only work for him a few days a week, and it doesn't pay enough to support my... Well, let's just say, my lifestyle. So I moonlight. The mayor's at his restaurant in town, *The Althea*, most days of the week. Sometimes he even conducts town business from the back room there."

"What type of restaurant is it?"

"Kind of New Age Mediterranean-style cuisine. You know, pastured farm-fresh eggs and local, grass-fed beef, organic sprouted quinoa with imported olive oil. That sort of thing."

"It sounds like the kind of place I'd eat at."

"Perhaps you'd allow me to take you to dinner there sometime."

She raised an eyebrow in surprise. "Maybe, if I'm in town long enough."

He gave her his winning smile, along with the Merlot. "What's a sophisticated woman like you, doing here in the first place?"

His smile distracted her for a moment, and all she could think to say was, "Circumstances. Isn't that why your girlfriend's back?"

"What girlfriend?"

"The one I saw you with at the Chinese restaurant."

"You mean, Krystal?" He shook his head. "She's just an old friend. There's only one man in this town she wants." He lifted his beer bottle toward Chad, who was setting more steaks on the grill.

Heather sipped her wine as she stared at their host, so cool and comfortable in his skin, like he had no conscience at all. The warm, sunny afternoon was going to get a whole lot warmer for him. "So what happened between Krystal and Chad, if you don't mind my asking?"

Derek moved his head from side to side in a slow motion. "Dunno. Their wedding was all set and paid for, and two weeks before, Chad calls it off and leaves town. Later I heard he moved to Chicago. He must've gotten cold feet. And Krystal... you never saw a woman so devastated. The next thing I heard, she was leaving for New York. And that was the end of that."

"But I saw them talking in Chad's car this morning."

"Last attempt at a reconciliation. She told me she'd try for one."

"Did she succeed?"

Derek spread his arms out wide. "Do you see her here?"

Krystal was nowhere to be seen. That didn't mean anything. Chad's personal life wasn't her concern, unless Krystal had paid him to kill her father. That could be another subject to pursue. Right now she was more interested in getting other information.

"It's such a tragedy about Krystal's dad. I guess by now, everyone knows my aunt's a suspect, but of course, she didn't do it. You were in the bar that night. Did one of the hotel guests buy a bottle of wine from you?"

Derek downed the rest of his beer. "Yeah, I told the police about it. A guy walked in, slapped a twenty on the bar and asked for a bottle of Zinfandel. I was too busy to get a good look at him. I just handed him the bottle and took the money. Hotel guests do it all the time. It's cheaper than drinking from the mini-bar in their rooms."

"Did anything stand out about this guy? Was he exceptionally tall or short? Did his clothes seem usual? Was he was wearing an old, gray overcoat on that warm night? Or maybe he was dressed as a member of the hotel staff?"

Derek grabbed another beer from the small refrigerator at the bar. "Hey, are there steaks being grilled here, or just me?"

He wasn't going to be much help. Heather turned to George Talan, who'd been listening to their conversation but trying to look like he wasn't. He folded his arms in front of him and turned his head in the other direction. "Don't look at me. I was out of town that night."

Heather searched for her aunt. Julia stooped near a lush rose garden a few feet away, searching for something. "Here kitty, kitty. What have you got there?"

The Willows' lean, black cat, Makki, amused himself by whacking at an object with his paw. Julia picked it up and dropped it like a hot frying pan.

Her derringer landed on the grass.

Chapter 14

HEATHER jumped to her feet. *It's Aunt Julia's gun.* Julia gave it a swift kick, as if she was trying to get it out of sight. Too late, everyone was already glancing her way.

"What is that?" George rushed over to inspect it. "It's a gun." He bent down to pick it up.

"No! Don't touch it," Heather cautioned.

George scrunched his eyes. "That's too small to be a real gun. It's probably just a kid's water pistol."

By then, everyone had gathered around it. "That's a real gun," Chad said. "I've seen one like it before. It's a derringer. Small but deadly."

Heather placed a hand on her hip. Things were looking worse for him. They both knew whose gun it was. How did *he* get it? "Why is that gun in your garden?"

"I don't know. Someone must have planted it here."

"Isn't it yours?" Derek raised an eyebrow as he stared at Julia. "I saw you with one just like it at the off-track betting parlor when you were there with Nikos Friday night."

Julia's jaw dropped open. "It's not mine. I never saw *that* gun before in my life."

Heather couldn't believe her ears. Loyalty prevented her from contradicting her aunt.

Chad picked up his cell phone. "I'll call the police. Let them deal with it."

Julia sauntered over to the grill and checked out the food sizzling there. She sniffed. "Smells great. I'm hungry. Let's eat before the police get here."

How can she be so cool? What was this, a condemned woman's last meal? Julia had merely said out loud what most people were probably thinking. Heather felt hungry herself at the moment. Hungry, and at the same time, a little sick.

After making the call, Chad shoved his cell back in his pocket and lifted a steak from the grill. Christine Talan, playing hostess, slipped a paper plate under it. She put a foil wrapped potato on the plate and handed it to Heather. "Please pass this to George, but don't let any of the food touch—he's very picky about that." She grabbed another plate, filled it, and gave it to Julia.

With all the plates distributed, everyone sat at the picnic table to eat. After a few bites of steak and a couple sips of wine, Heather's stomach settled down a bit. But it wasn't long before the whirr of a squad car siren came from the front of the house, and her stomach was once again up in the air.

Everyone continued to eat as Detective Lindsey approached the table. And why shouldn't they? None of them had anything to fear from the police, except her aunt. Unless one of them was the murderer.

The detective glanced at the plates. "Steak?"

Chad stood. "I'll be glad to grill one for you."

"Maybe later. Show me what you found."

Julia turned an anxious glance at Heather. She pushed her plate, with its half-eaten steak, aside and alternately chewed her thumb nail and sipped from her glass of Merlot.

Heather continued to eat. Although she was going through the motions, her delicious-looking steak, grilled to a medium-rare perfection, tasted like cardboard.

Detective Lindsey put the gun in an evidence bag and walked back to the table. "Ballistics should tell me if this derringer is the murder weapon after they do some testing. Who found the gun?"

Chad turned to look at the cat, who was sniffing at Ashley's plate from his perch on her lap. "Makki did."

"Your cat found it?"

"He was wandering around the rose garden and must have thought it was a toy. He swatted at it."

The detective gave everyone at the table a quick glance. "Anyone else see this cat playing with the gun?"

"I took it away from him," Julia said.

Detective Lindsey put a hand on Julia's shoulder. "Are you sure you weren't the one who dropped it there?"

Julia straightened as if a rod had been shoved up her spine. She stared at his hand. "No. I did *not* put it there. And kindly take your hand off me."

"I'm going to have to take you down to the station, Miss Fairchild."

Julia glanced up at him. "You can't arrest me. I haven't done anything."

The detective's stone-cold expression didn't waver. "I'm taking you in because there's a bench warrant out in your name for numerous unpaid traffic violations."

Heather had forgotten about those.

The detective pulled out a set of handcuffs. Chad walked up to him. "You won't have to put those on her. I'm sure she'll go quietly."

Julia stood with a frown. She grabbed her glass, chugged her Merlot, and checked inside her purse. "Heather, get me some peppermints... and a traffic ticket lawyer."

Heather followed them to the front of the house as everyone crowded around her. After the patrol car left, they all started toward the yard. Heather lagged behind. "Does anyone know a good 'ticket' lawyer?"

Christine stopped and turned to face her. "Don't worry." She glanced over her shoulder. "Maybe we can find one for her. What do you think, George?"

"Stop sticking your nose into other people's business," he said. "I'm sure Heather can handle it herself."

Christine tilted her head to the side, and shuffled back to the yard. "I'm just trying to help."

Chad put an arm around Heather's shoulders. She shrugged it off. *That hypocrite, acting so supportive.*

"I'm sorry," he said. "I know you're upset. There's nothing you can do for your aunt right now. They'll probably book her on misdemeanor charges and put her in a holding cell overnight. The judge will be at the courthouse in the morning, and she'll most likely just have to pay the fines. I mean, how many parking tickets can she possibly have, two or three?"

"It's a lot more than that. What if she can't pay the fines?"

Chad raised his eyebrows. "If she can't, she might be sentenced to jail time, or more likely, community service hours. I'm pretty sure I can find her a traffic ticket lawyer she can consult with, pro bono."

"Oh, I'm sure you can." Her words came out sounding slightly more sarcastic than she'd intended, and really ungrateful, but she couldn't help it.

"What do you mean by that?"

"I know which lawyers you worked for in Chicago. And I know what you've been doing!"

He looked at her as if she was crazy. "What are you talking about?"

A flash of red shot across her eyes. *Come on! Drop the act.* She shook a finger at him. "Yoouuu know."

Storming off, she got into her car, but it was impossible to drive until her head stopped pounding and her heartbeat slowed. She'd lost her cool… again. All the anger and hostility she'd been harboring against Jack came pouring out. Only this time, to her horror, her logic sounded just like her aunt's.

Taking deep breaths, she leaned her head against the steering wheel in an effort to relax. Knuckles tapped on her window.

A man's muffled voice said, "Will you please come in the house and talk to me?"

Heat flushed her cheeks. "No." She cranked the engine and put the air on to cool her face and drown out his words.

The passenger door opened. Chad got in. "Then we can talk here."

Her stomach clenched. "I have nothing to say to you.... You..." *Two-faced con man.*

"I can't help if you won't talk to me."

"Why should I?" *So you can report my every move to Jack?*

"Because you came to me for advice, remember?"

That was before I knew who you were working for

"Now things have gotten worse for your aunt, and you're carrying a load of problems on your shoulders you might not be able to handle alone."

You have no idea.

Chad put a warm hand on hers. "You've already told me about your aunt being suspected of murder, and I pretty much guessed the Derringer was hers. That gun had to be planted in my yard by the murderer. The police will eventually find out it's your aunt's, and she'll need to consult a *criminal* lawyer."

Why did people always state the obvious? "Really, do you think?" Her remark came out exactly as she intended, with just the right amount of sarcasm.

He released her hand, opened the car door, and stepped out. "Okay, if you don't want my help, that's fine." He slammed the door and marched back toward the yard.

"Fine!" She had to have the last word on that. With her lips pressed in a tight grimace, Heather put the car in gear and careened out of his driveway.

***

The police station was just as Heather had imaged it: A one story, nondescript, brown brick building with bars on the windows. A carved wood *Willow's Bend Police* sign hung above the front door.

She drove around the back to the parking lot just as the officer was walking her aunt inside. She followed. Julia glanced over her shoulder, no doubt to see if Heather was there for support. Heather waved and forced a small smile.

Inside, the officer led Julia to a back room. When Heather got near the door, a tall, brawny officer with the name Henderson on his uniform stepped in front of her. "You can't go in there."

He was the officer stationed at the front door of the hotel. Chad called him Sam. She hoped he remembered her. "You've arrested my aunt for traffic warrants, and I need to find out what's going to happen to her."

"She'll be booked and will have to spend the night in a cell. Tomorrow morning, the judge will pass sentence."

"Can I at least visit the poor woman? She must be scared to death."

"Don't worry." Officer Hendricks's voice was kind. "I'm sure the arresting officer will be as gentle as he can. Just give him fifteen minutes for the booking process. Once she's settled, I'll let you see her."

"Thanks."

Heather left the station and drove to the drug store to buy her aunt some peppermints. She wandered around and glanced at items she really didn't need, just to waste time. It was the longest fifteen minutes she'd ever spent.

Back at the station, Heather followed Officer Hendricks through a narrow hall that led to several jail cells. The place looked clean, but a faint scent of urine saturated the air. The cracks in the walls had been re-plastered and re-painted a dark green more than once.

Most of the cells were empty, except for her aunt and a bearded, middle-aged man in the cell across from her, sleeping. The area smelled of beer and whisky.

Heather pointed to the man. "Who's that?"

"Just one of our homeless," the officer answered. "He lives on Bleaker Street down the block from the pawn shop. This time he's sleeping off a bender. I don't know where he got the money for hard liquor when he doesn't have money for food most of the time."

As Heather approached her cell, Julia jumped from the bed and shoved her arms out of the cell bars. "Am I ever glad to see you. Thanks for coming. Did you bring me some peppermints? I can't stand the smell in this place."

Heather glanced at the officer standing a few feet away. "I had to check my purse at the front desk."

"Don't tell me you don't have anything." Julia put her arms down, and her shoulders dropped. Heather moved close to the bars and handed her a tiny box.

Officer Henderson glanced over at them. "What did you give her?"

"Just a box of mints."

He put his hand out. "Let's have it."

Julia shoved her arm out of the bars and showed him the box, her lips pressed into a tight frown. "What kind of a human being are you when you won't let a poor old lady have a box of peppermints?" She sniffled. "If you don't let me keep these..." She gritted her teeth in barely restrained anger. "I'll tell the media about how cruelly I was treated, and your whole department will be so embarrassed, it'll take *years* to live it down."

The officer took a few steps back and put his hands out in a defensive stance. "Okay lady, keep the mints."

"And one more thing," Julia said. "Can you make that guy in the cell over there stop snoring? Or get me a set of earplugs."

He shook his head as he walked down the hallway toward the front office.

Julia pressed the mints to her nose and took a long whiff. Her eyes half-closed. Evidently, one smell was enough to calm her. Heather could only wonder what else her aunt demanded from the officer.

"Have you been giving the police a hard time?"

"You have to take the upper hand in every situation. Otherwise men will walk all over you, whether they're the police or not."

"Take it easy on them. No one is walking all over you. A reliable source told me court will be in session tomorrow morning, and you'll be appearing before the judge. You'll most likely get probation if you can come up with the money to pay your fines, or else you may have to do some community service time."

Julia opened the box, popped a mint into her mouth, and took a deep breath. "I know," she said in a matter-of-fact tone. "I was arrested a couple years ago for passing bad checks when I lived with a real estate agent for a while. The rat emptied my bank account. I honestly thought I had the money to cover those checks."

She glanced around. "The Federal prison was much cleaner than this dump."

Heather's jaw dropped open. *This must be the "just one more thing" she neglected to tell me.*

***

In her hotel room, Heather switched on her laptop to find out when traffic court would convene in the morning. There was no way of knowing when her aunt would appear before the judge, she'd just have to sit in the courtroom and wait.

She'd better find out how much money she could scrape together, today. There was only around five hundred she could get in cash from her credit card—it was near the limit. She dug her cell from her purse and called Emily.

Her sister picked up on the second ring.

"Hi, it's Heather. Aunt Julia's been arrested."

Emily sucked in a breath. "What is it this time?"

She must've known about the bad check fiasco. "Unpaid parking tickets."

Emily let the breath out. "Oh, I thought she'd been arrested for murder. Why am I not surprised at the irresponsibility of that woman? So what happens now?"

"I'm going to the courthouse tomorrow morning to find out how much she owes. I'll try to scrape up the money to help her pay the tickets and the fines."

"Why do you bother with her when you have problems of your own?"

Heather couldn't believe how callous her sister was toward their aunt. "Because I owe her. She stuck by Mom when Dad left. You were away at college, but I was at home when Mom had her breakdown. I couldn't have gotten through it without Aunt Julia there for support. I can't let her down, now. Do you think Mom would help?"

"Mom doesn't have any real money. So I doubt it. And I've already done my part. I got her a nice job and dibs on a decent place to live. I can't afford to do any more for her. An assistant professor doesn't make very much, so you're on your own."

"How about Uncle Gordon? He's *swimming* in money. Do you think he'd kick in a few dollars to help his sister?"

Emily chuckled. "Are you kidding? He wouldn't even help Mom, and he *likes* her."

"Do you know of anyone else?"

"Don't even think about asking Dad. You could always try Jack. I'm sure he'd be happy to help. The man's called me a dozen times since Friday night. He really wants you to forgive him. Or you could kiss up to your boss to get your old job back."

I knew she'd get around to suggesting those options. "And be indebted to either of them for the rest of my life? Not if they were the last two men on this planet."

"Well, maybe Aunt Julia's better off in jail. At least it'll keep her out of trouble."

"Somehow, I doubt that."

A muffled voice sounded over the phone. "Gotta go. John and I are about to walk into a Mozart concert in the park, and I've got to turn this off. Keep me informed if things get any worse."

Knowing Aunt Julia, they probably will.

Heather ended the call and rubbed her thumbnail along the length of her bottom lip. She plopped down on the bed. As she lay there thinking of a way to help her aunt, drowsiness crept over her. Heather told herself she wouldn't go to sleep, but stress, coupled with that glass of wine she drank on a nearly empty stomach, won out, and before long, she dozed off.

A ringing sound woke her.

Chapter 15

HEATHER jumped out of bed and glanced around to find out what could possibly be making the noise. Her cell had a melodious tone she recognized right away, so that wasn't it. Disoriented at first, it finally dawned on her it had to be the hotel phone. Who would be calling her here on *that* phone?

She picked up the receiver and, in a cautious voice, said, "Hello."

A man's voice responded. "Hi Heather. Did I wake you?"

She cleared her throat. "No, not at all," she lied. "Who is this?"

"It's Derek."

"Oh, hi." *Why is he calling me at...?* She checked the clock. *Six-thirty.*

"Since you didn't eat much at the barbecue this afternoon, I thought you might want to join me for dinner."

She didn't know what to say, so she didn't say anything.

"I'm going to *The Athena Restaurant.* You mentioned you'd like to go there sometime, so I thought tonight could be good. I mean, after what happened this afternoon, I figured you might be hungry and could use some company."

It's kind of last minute, but I do need to eat, and I'm not crazy about spending any more time in this room alone. "Sure. I'd love to."

"Great. I'll pick you up in an hour."

"No. I'll meet you there."

She hung up and checked out the restaurant on her laptop. Business casual. Good, because that's all she'd brought with her. And it was only a five minute drive from the hotel. That gave her time to take a quick shower and change.

***

After dressing, Heather got into her car and set the GPS for the restaurant. The buildings in the part of town where *The Athena* was located were newer, and the store fronts had a modern look to them, with more up-to-date names.

She'd expected to see a Greek amphitheater-style building, but the restaurant was a buff brick and clear glass structure. Derek stood near the front door, wearing jeans with a dark sports jacket over a crisp white shirt. His dark eyes gave her a slow once-over as she approached him from the parking lot.

"You look gorgeous."

She glanced down at her pale green, short summer dress. "Thanks."

"So, what do you think of the place?"

"It looks nice. I'll reserve judgment until I taste the food."

He opened the door for her. White linen cloths on wood tables, stiff-backed chairs with aubergine fabric cushions, furniture positioned a little too close together—it was the same as many of the newer restaurants she'd eaten at lately.

Although the room was crowded, they were immediately shown to a cozy-looking table in a corner of the austere restaurant. A waiter in a white coat approached them, carrying a silver ice bucket that held a bottle of *Domaine Chandon.*

Champagne was one of the few things she and Jack had in common, so she'd tasted a lot, from the worst to the best. This one, although not expensive, was good.

Derek's lips curved into a small smile. "I hope you don't mind. I ordered this ahead of time."

"Not at all. I love champagne." *What I really mind is men who think they know what I want.*

She put a hand over her glass. "But not tonight. I'm driving. I'll just have a glass of sparkling water with a twist of lemon."

The waiter raised an eyebrow and stared at Derek, who stared right back.

"Very good." The waiter set the bottle in the ice bucket and walked away. Derek filled his flute and raised it. "To a woman who knows what she wants." He took a sip.

The waiter returned with the water and handed each a dinner menu. Heather scanned it. Everything sounded appetizing. She couldn't help the guilt that tugged at her heart. "I'm a little ashamed being in this lovely restaurant and ordering from a delectable menu when my aunt is in a jail cell. I can't imagine what she's having for dinner."

"Actually, Christine Talan is bringing her a home-cooked meal. She's a great cook. I arranged it with the police. They usually give their detainees a hamburger from The Club Car Diner."

"How thoughtful."

"It was nothing."

"Have you known the Talans long?"

Derek put his menu down. "Just since we moved here when I was a senior in high school. But I'd rather talk about you. Where did you get those stunning hazel eyes?"

Why do men ask questions that are impossible to answer? Now, she couldn't look at him, so she gazed at the silver framed picture on the wall to her right: a jockey dressed in bright blue silks, standing next to a chestnut race horse.

When she didn't answer his question, Derek said, "I hope you're not in a serious relationship at the moment."

"If I was, I wouldn't be here." *What kind of woman does he think I am?*

"Great. Because I'm available right now too, and I thought you and I could get a little better acquainted."

"You realize that as soon as this business with my aunt is cleared up, we're leaving town."

"Too bad." Derek leaned back in his seat. "You're such a refreshing change from all the crazy people I have to contend with every day. Is there anything I can do or say to convince you to stay?"

"I don't know. Is there?"

A moment of silence passed between them. No doubt Derek was trying to come up with an answer. Time for a change of subject.

Heather looked around the restaurant and pointed to the framed photo on the wall. "That's an unusual picture for a restaurant wall. It's different from the landscapes on the other walls."

Derek's gaze followed hers. "That's the winner of the Belmont Stakes ten years ago. The mayor won enough money to open this place. Of course, he wasn't the mayor then. He was down to his last few dollars when he bet on that long-shot and won. Nikos wasn't happy about paying out that much money."

"I can imagine."

"After the race, he quit gambling cold turkey. He keeps this picture on the wall as a reminder."

"You must know the mayor well."

"Besides working in his office, part-time, my dad's on the city council." Derek leaned forward and dropped his voice. "Don't tell anyone you heard it from me, but he's getting his campaign together to run against Mayor Bandik in the next election."

"I won't say a word."

Their waiter appeared at the table, startling Heather. "Are you ready to order?"

"Yes." She handed him her menu. "I'll have the grilled salmon salad."

Derek ordered the lamb.

After the waiter left, as a favor to her aunt, Heather asked, "I know this sounds insensitive in view of the situation with Nikos, but do you think Krystal will keep her father's business open with the Kentucky Derby coming up next weekend?"

Derek stared at her and took a slow, deliberate sip of champagne, as if he was considering what to say. He toyed with his glass for a long moment. "Since her dad's funeral is Wednesday, Krystal told me she's thinking of doing a grand re-opening to coincide with The Derby on Saturday. She's considering quitting her job and taking over the business permanently, especially now that Chad's back in town."

A slight twinge crossed Heather's heart. She didn't know why that information should bother her.

Derek tipped his glass in her direction. "Are you're interested in picking a horse to bet on in the Derby?"

"Who me? I don't even know what to look for when I see a horse."

"I'll be glad to help you make a decision. I've laid down my share of bets over the years and done pretty well."

"Thanks. I'll keep that in mind when Derby Day rolls around." *Not that I have any disposable income to bet with right now.* She picked up her glass to take a sip of water, and her peripheral vision caught a glimpse of someone familiar. The man put his hand against the door and gave it a push as he glanced at her over his shoulder.

"What do you know about that man leaving the restaurant?"

He turned to look. "Why are you interested?"

That's a legitimate question. I'll just have to trust him. "I believe he's Nikos's former bookkeeper. I saw him with Dutch, from the day spa, at the Chinese restaurant this afternoon. My aunt told me both of them had an argument with Nikos the evening before he was killed. She thought it might have been about money."

"Johnny Tanner was the one friend Nikos could always rely on."

"So, as his bookkeeper, Tanner was at the heart of everything."

"Yeah, and he also likes to play the horses. Don't get me started on Dutch, who owed Nikos big time. Horseplayers are a funny breed. They were his pals as long as they were winning, but when they were on a losing streak, he was their enemy."

"Did Nikos have a lot of enemies, I mean, anyone who might want to kill him?"

Derek scrunched his eyebrows. "You working for the DA, now?"

She gave a nervous laugh. "No. What I want to do is to figure out if there were any other viable suspects, besides my aunt, who wanted to kill Nikos."

Derek put his elbow on the table and rested his chin on his hand. "And speaking of your aunt, at the barbecue this afternoon, you said circumstances brought you to this town. What circumstances?"

Heather ran her index finger around the rim of her glass as she considered how much to tell him. "I was on my way to visit my sister, when I had to get off the train here. I ran into my aunt unexpectedly, and you pretty much know the rest."

He gave her an endearing smile. "Guess I'll always be grateful to the railroad for bringing you here."

The waiter set their dinners on the table. While they ate, the conversation lapsed into silence except for the occasional comment about the excellence of the food. But Heather was also filled with concerns about her aunt's situation. Since Derek worked in the mayor's office, maybe he could help keep Julia out of prison.

While he was extremely attractive, she didn't think stringing the guy along was fair because she had no intentions of staying here. But like Aunt Julia said, *sometimes you have to do the wrong thing at the right time to get what you need.*

With the meal over, the waiter came to their table and set down two cups of coffee. She poured cream in her cup and took a cautious sip. Over the rim, she spotted Chad walking in the door. Derek turned to see who she was staring at.

"What's he doing here?" they said simultaneously.

She and Derek looked at each other. It was Derek who broke the silence. "That's what I get for asking Chad if you two were a couple. When he said no, it wouldn't take much for him to guess I'd ask you out for dinner. And this is the only decent restaurant in town."

Derek took a sip of black coffee and glared at Chad, who was now scanning the room. "But for someone who didn't seem interested... it makes me wonder." He tapped his index finger on the hard edge of the table.

Heather's face burned. She didn't have to wonder why Chad was here. Now he could report to Jack that he'd seen her on a dinner date with another man. *Good!* It was payback time, even though she didn't consider this a real date, more like a fact-finding mission.

Chad caught her gaze. She stared right back and took an awkward sip of coffee. A few drops dripped down her chin. She grabbed a napkin to blot her face and turned to Derek with an embarrassed smile. He stared off in the distance with one eyebrow raised and his lips pressed in a tight line.

Heather opened her mouth to continue their conversation, but it was suddenly difficult to make small talk.

Uncomfortable with Chad gawking at her, which might possibly go on for as long as she stayed in this restaurant, she stood. "Thank you very much for this delicious dinner, Derek." She checked her watch. "I really have to be going."

"You haven't even finished your coffee, and I was hoping we could go to a movie later."

"Sorry, not tonight. I'll take a rain-check."

She didn't hang around to hear his response. Instead, she grabbed her purse, stalked past Chad, and headed out the door with her head high and her gaze straight ahead, completely ignoring his intense stare.

Did that seem rude? Probably. But she had to get out of there. Her steps increased in speed as she made her way down the sidewalk toward the parking lot. Another set of footsteps echoed in the dark, behind her. Heart racing, Heather shoved her hand in her shoulder bag and pulled out her pepper spray along with her car key. She hit the unlock button.

The footsteps got louder, more rushed.

Reaching the car, her hand trembled as she yanked the door open and jumped into the driver's seat. As the steps approached, she slammed the door and hit the lock.

Chapter 16

THE footsteps passed by without stopping. A breath of relief escaped her lips as her heartbeat slowed. She gazed out the driver's side window at a man with stooped shoulders shrouded in a gray, stained, and ragged raincoat heading toward the next block. He held an over-stuffed, brown paper shopping bag in each hand, his salt and pepper hair flying wild in the breeze. There was something about him that made her think she'd seen him before.

A little disheartened neither Chad nor Derek had come after her, Heather started the car. As she sat, staring into the distant night sky, it came to her. *Of course, he's the homeless guy who was sleeping off a bender in the cell across from Aunt Julia.*

Driving back to the hotel, her heart sank a little more. Too bad it wasn't Chad who'd followed her out to the parking lot. She'd love to have a confrontation with him about Jack right now, just to get her suspicions out in the open. And then he'd finally have to admit everything.

As she stepped into the hotel lobby. Christine Talan waved her over to the front desk. She pointed to a crystal vase with two dozen roses attractively displayed.

"Someone sent these to you." She handed Heather a small card in a florist's envelope.

Heather recognized Jack's handwriting. His first step in trying to soften her up always started with roses. She wasn't falling for it anymore. "Do you have a pen I can borrow?"

Christine handed her a pen bearing the hotel's logo.

Heather printed the word, refused, in large, block letters across the card. "Please send these back to the florist who delivered them."

"Aren't you going to open the card?"

"I know who it's from."

Christine sniffed a rose. "You must really hate the sender."

"That's not a strong enough word for how I feel about him." Heather checked the wall clock. "I didn't think you'd be working this late."

"Sometimes I switch with the night clerk. My husband's on the road for a couple of days. He left right after dinner, and I don't like to spend the night in that big house alone. Too many scary noises. I've always thought it was haunted."

"Don't you have friends or family you can stay with or who can stay with you?"

"My kids are all grown and moved away. I hate to impose on friends. This works out better for me. I'm not alone, and I make extra spending money."

"We can all use a little extra money." *I could sure use some right now.*

Christine eyed Heather's appearance. "You look very nice. Are you coming back from visiting with your aunt?"

"No. I just had dinner with Derek Kane. He told me he'd arranged for you to bring my aunt a home-cooked meal. Thank you. I'm sure she appreciated it."

"He arranged it?" Christine grumbled. "Well, I guess he did by paving the way with the police chief. It was originally Chad's idea."

"I see. So Derek just took the credit. Guess he's trying to make himself look good." *Typical man.*

"Since you're new here, let me give you a little friendly advice. You could do a lot worse than Derek Kane. But just remember that he's broken a few hearts."

"I can imagine. I found him very charming."

"Oh, he is. And that smile..." Christine sighed. "That's the problem with men like him. Too darn handsome for their own good."

Jack came to mind. And Chad. "From what I hear, he's not the only one who's broken hearts. Krystal Stamos's, for instance?"

A frown crossed Christine's lips as she furrowed her brow. "That was a sad case. Chad was pretty broken up about what happened, too. The poor man. This is just my opinion, but I think he's hiding a deep hurt. What he needs is someone to love. And now that he's back in town, I'm going to make it my mission to find him someone special."

She was dying to ask what really happened to break up Chad and Krystal, but for some odd reason, she couldn't. "Won't interfering in Chad's love life upset your husband?"

"What George doesn't know won't bother him." Christine winked. "Don't tell him I told you that."

Heather made a zipping motion across her lips.

"And speaking of your aunt," Christine continued, "She and I had a nice talk while she ate her dinner. I don't believe, for one minute, that she killed Nikos."

"Thanks for the vote of confidence."

"She's a remarkable woman in many ways, and she's had such an interesting life. Julia's seen and done so many things I wish I could have."

"Unfortunately, not all of them within the law."

Christine let out a chuckle. "I can understand that. She was a woman alone in the world. And she attracted some bad men who took advantage of her."

More like she took advantage of them.

"You can't help who you're attracted to, can you?"

"You're right. You can't." Heather still couldn't understand her attraction for Chad over Derek.

The hotel telephone rang. Christine picked up the receiver, but before she answered the call, she said, "If you need anything, just let me know."

"Thanks." Heather left the lobby and walked toward the hotel bar. She needed a nightcap to come to grips with what Christine told her about Derek. *Too darn handsome for his own good.* That described so many men she knew. And she had to admit, Derek could make any woman fall for him with that smile.

She ordered a small brandy at the bar and took her drink to an empty table in the corner of the room. It wasn't as if Derek was the first man she'd met who'd broken a lot of hearts. *Ugh!* She sipped her brandy and cringed at the thought of being drawn to that type of man, again.

***

Sleepy from the brandy, but listless from the nap she'd taken earlier, Heather tossed in bed unable to get comfortable. Her mind raced with the events of the day and finally came back to her own life. She really should update her resume and send it out. Just because her aunt's life was on hold right now didn't mean hers should be too.

But why would any executives want her on their team after they'd checked with her previous boss? He probably thought she was out of her mind for busting into his office like that, screaming at him—and rage quitting. Things looked pretty grim for her job-wise.

Heather's stomach churned as her thoughts raced. She swallowed to moisten her dry mouth. Getting out of bed, she flicked on the light and headed toward the desk for a bottle of water. A squeaking noise in the hall distracted her.

Straining her ear against the door, she listened. Not a sound. Then footfalls and the telltale creak of floor-boards. Then silence again—a silence so complete, she began to doubt her own ears. She checked the peep-hole. No one there.

Her curiosity got the better of her. She opened the door and stuck her head out. Another squeak and the shadow of a man rounding the corner. Heather pulled her head in and closed and locked the door.

As far as she knew, only one other room on this floor was occupied, and there were two women in it. Maybe a new guest had checked in.

I'll look into it first thing tomorrow.

Chapter 17

MORNING was punctuated by the buzzing noise Heather had learned to dread. Tired from not having slept most of the night, she rolled over and turned off the alarm.

The day dawned ahead of her, uninviting and empty. This was the first Monday in years she didn't have to rush to the office to work on a backlog of projects before meeting with a client. All she had planned for the day was to get to the courthouse and await her aunt's appearance before the judge.

It was still early, so she closed her eyes for a few more minutes.

The door clicked.

Heather jerked awake. She shot up, bolt-straight, her heart racing.

Julia sauntered in.

Heather put a hand on her chest and blinked the sleep away. "What are you doing here? You were supposed to appear before the judge today."

"Thanks, it's nice to see you, too." Julia let out a long whoosh as if she was out of breath.

Heather jumped out of bed. "I'm sorry, I didn't mean it to sound as if I didn't care, I mean..."

Julia waved Heather's words away. "I know what you mean. I don't really know what happened. After Christine left the jail this morning with my breakfast dishes— she's such a thoughtful lady, bringing me home-cooked meals and staying with me while I ate —an officer came to my cell, unlocked the door, and said my fines were paid, and I was free to go. When I collected my purse at the front desk, another officer said I couldn't leave town because I had to start my community service tomorrow morning." Julia handed Heather a business card.

Heather looked it over, read the name of the supervisor, and handed it back. "Who'd have the power to do something like that?"

"Someone who knows the judge, and called in a favor?"

"It would have to be. *Could it have been Derek?* Do you have any idea who paid your fines?"

Julia shoved her hands through her messy red hair, making it messier. "I think I do. When I was locked up, I demanded to have my one phone call. But instead of calling you, I called your ex-uncle, Stan. I think maybe he paid the fines."

"How much did he have to fork over?"

"Oh, I don't know, somewhere in excess of two thousand dollars, I believe."

"Are... are you joking? Heather stammered.

Julia put two hands up in her defense. "Some of the counties in Illinois tacked on ridiculously high fines for neglecting to pay those tickets. And of course, I'm going to reimburse Stan for every penny."

"How are you going to do that? You might have to do community service for eight hours a day, seven days a week for months. Do you even know how many hours you have to put in?"

"Not yet. From what I understand, someone will notify me."

"When you do find out, I have a feeling it will pretty much rule out getting a job."

Julia moaned. "With no job, I won't be able to afford a place to stay." She collapsed onto the bed. "I'll have to live in the street like the homeless while I serve out my sentence." She put a hand on the small of her back and groaned. Her eyes widened with the scared rabbit look she did so well. "I can't do that! I have back problems, and sleeping on a cardboard box in the street would kill me. Not to mention the lice!" Her wild gaze darted around the room.

"How much gas is in your rental car right now?"

Heather grabbed the keys, dropped them into her purse and zipped it shut. She placed a hand on her aunt's shoulder to calm her.

"I know you're finding this hard to deal with. I am too. Don't even think about running. We'll come up with something, even if I have find a way to support you while you're picking up trash or whatever they'll have you doing."

Julia dropped her shoulders. "Thanks. I knew I could count on... What do you mean, *find a way* to support me? Your mom said you have a *great* job and live in a fabulous condo you share with your rich boyfriend."

Not anymore. Heather rubbed her temples as a stalling tactic. She'd have to tell her aunt the situation sooner or later, and now would probably be the best time, before she counted on her generosity a little too much and would eventually be disappointed.

"Actually, I don't have either. I quit my 'so-called' wonderful job last Friday afternoon. It became impossible. I couldn't deal with the stress. And as far as Jack is concerned... you were right when you said he had a roving eye. I wouldn't accept it for a long time, but I've finally come to my senses and have left him for good."

Julia's eyebrows raised as her brown eyes flew wide open. "Don't say that. Not even in jest!"

"I wouldn't joke at a time like this." Heather lowered her head and waited for a heated reaction from her aunt. *I should have told her sooner.*

Julia's eyebrows relaxed. "Oh dear. This is sad." She stood and put an arm around Heather's shoulders. "You keep telling me not to run. Isn't that exactly what you're doing? I see a lot of myself in you. I was about your age, maybe a year or two younger, when I first ran from a situation I couldn't deal with any longer. And the circumstances were almost exactly the same as yours. Why do you think your Uncle Stan remarried so quickly after our divorce?"

"Sorry, I didn't know. But I don't see the parallel. Leaving a toxic relationship and a stressful job are not the same as running away from my problems."

Julia took her arm down. A slow smile spread across her lips.

Heather had to wonder if her aunt was making some kind of connection between the two of them. She couldn't imagine what that could be. *My situation isn't like hers at all. I've always faced my problems. These just happened to be a little overwhelming.*

Julia opened her suitcase, collected a robe, and slipped off her shoes. She headed toward the bathroom. As her hand clutched the doorknob, she squared her shoulders. "I'm taking a hot, scented bubble bath to soak off the smell of jail."

Her aunt was calm and reasonable—and that was what was so worrisome. She could deal with a mood —a mood was bound to pass. But a calm and reasonable reaction after the heat of panic is very different. Heather closed her eyes and tilted her head back. She hoped Aunt Julia hadn't concocted some half-baked scheme to escape her responsibilities because she thought that's what Heather was doing.

I'd better stick around the room for a while.

Heather dressed in a tank-top and jean shorts, brushed her hair up into a pony tail, and twisted it into a top-knot, securing it with hair pins. She wanted to keep it off her neck while she spent a few hours at the day spa's gym to work out, and possibly find more useful information about the former wrestler who ran it. Her aunt didn't need a murder charge on top of everything else she had to cope with.

Heather signed on her laptop. Her resume didn't take long to update, and she was finally able to send it out. Reading and answering her emails was another matter.

Twenty minutes later, Julia rushed out of the bathroom, pulling on a rumpled white silk kimono, embroidered with huge blue peacocks. Excitement lit up her eyes. "I've been so upset about everything, I almost forgot to tell you. When they let out the homeless guy, I got a glimpse of his face and recognized him as the room service guy who delivered my wine."

Heather looked up from the computer. "Are you sure?"

"Pretty sure." Julia bit her bottom lip. "I can't be one hundred percent. I mean, he'd cleaned up. But with those stooped shoulders and that gray hair, I wouldn't rule him out."

"Did you tell a police officer?"

"I did."

"What did he say?"

"He said they'd look into it."

Heather grabbed her cell. "I'll call Detective Lindsey, just to make sure he knows the homeless man should be questioned. He might have been paid to deliver that wine to your room. Or he could be another suspect."

"Let's hope so." Julia threw her soiled clothes in a heap on the floor. "I'm tired of being on the spot. I just want this whole thing to go away." She pulled off her spread and plopped onto the bed. "So much has happened. I feel like I've walked about fifteen miles instead of having done nothing but sit in that cell."

Heather made the call. The detective thanked her for the information and assured her he was following every lead. Things were looking up. She continued scrolling through her social media websites, where she blocked Jack and everyone associated with him. She deleted all his pictures from her phone and everywhere else she could find them.

It didn't take long before Julia's snoring disturbed her concentration. She left her aunt a sticky note to let her know where she'd be, closed the laptop, grabbed her purse, and headed toward the door. The room telephone rang. She about-faced and leaped to pick up the receiver on the second ring before it could wake her aunt.

"Hello."

"This is the front desk. A package just came for you, Miss Stanton."

"Thanks, I'll be down in a minute."

When she reached the lobby, the desk clerk handed Heather a small FedEx box with a return label from Tiffany.

Excited, Heather took the package to a side table and ripped it open. *Why would I be getting a package from Tiffany?* She unraveled the white bow on the turquoise box inside, and opened it. Gasping, she pulled out the white gold, 2 karat, diamond solitaire pendant she'd been admiring in their window for the past few months. "It's gorgeous."

Then it dawned on her. She didn't have to read the card. *Jack's the only one I've ever told about this necklace. It must be another attempt to win me back.* She rushed to repack the box, and went to the desk clerk. "Could you please tell me where the nearest Fedex store is?"

***

After dropping off the box, Heather walked to the gym. A toned, young woman with platinum blond hair manned the front desk. "Can I help you?"

"Do I need a membership to use your gym?"

"You do, but a year's membership comes with a two-week free trial, after which you can cancel."

She'd be cancelling it well within that time-frame. After she signed up, Heather sauntered around to familiarize herself with the equipment. She walked on a treadmill for a few minutes, got off, picked up a six-pound weight in each hand, and did a few reps before putting them back on the rack. Across from the weights was just what she needed—a stationary bike to firm up her slightly out of shape thigh muscles.

The bike was across from the gym's office, where large glass windows showed a clear view of Dutch seated in a swivel chair, holding a cell phone to his ear. She couldn't take her eyes off his physique.

With those enormous muscles, he wouldn't require a gun to kill someone. A couple of well-placed punches would be all he needed.

The door to the office stood slightly ajar, so as she approached the bikes, she stopped in front and bent down, pretending to tie her shoelace while she eavesdropped.

"This has to end. Now!" A few moments later, "No. It's what you do when you're in love, stupid."

Heather stood, jumped onto the nearest bike, and pedaled her heart out. After the sixth time around the electronic track, her thighs ached so much she had to slow her pace to a crawl for the next lap. Struggling to catch her breath, she averted her eyes as Dutch left the office and made his way toward the juice bar.

She could use some juice right now, but first she'd have a look around his office. Heather stopped the bike and wiped the perspiration from her forehead with a paper towel from the dispenser, and pulled another to wipe down the seat. She massaged her sore thighs until he was out of sight. With wobbly legs, she made her way to the office door and surveyed the gym.

Only two people walked on the treadmills, and they were occupied with the electronic data in front of them, so she stepped in. Rushing to his desk, she checked the computer screen. His desktop was loaded with icons. There wasn't time to figure out what she needed to open to get any pertinent information.

She pulled the top desk drawer open. Calculator, sunglasses, tape, paperclips, pens. She shut it and stooped down. A file drawer? Who kept paper files these days? Dutch evidently didn't. It was jammed full of sample packets of protein powder and bottles of water. She stood, nudging the drawer closed with her knee.

This was getting her nowhere. Maybe it would be easier to get information if she just made his acquaintance and had a nice, straightforward conversation with him. She walked out and headed toward the juice bar.

And there the tall hulk of a man stood, sipping from a clear glass containing forest-green liquid and wearing a white tee with the words *Willows Wellness Center and*

Day Spa sprawled across his bulging chest. Every defined muscle of his derriere was squeezed into tight, black spandex shorts.

Heather perused the menu on the board behind his head as his bear-like eyes gave her the once-over. "What'll it be?"

Tough decision. So many things she never heard of, much less tasted. "I don't know. What would you suggest?"

"I think you might enjoy something light and on the sweet side with a little punch to it. How about a mixture of tropical fruit juice with protein powder and a good dash of Noni for stamina? You look like you could use it."

"Are you referring to my short stint on the stationary bike?" She didn't think he noticed her.

"It didn't take long before you were winded."

He opened a protein powder packet like the one she'd seen in his desk, added it, along with the other ingredients, to the blender, and turned it on.

She waited until he turned it off. "I'm a little out of practice at the moment."

"Well, if you want to work here, you're going to have to tone up. I mean, you're in pretty good shape, but... " He walked around the bar to stand behind her. She glanced over her shoulder as he clutched his thighs. "Ya know?"

"It's kind of rude to point that out." She knew what he meant.

"Not at all. It's my job to tell people what part of their bodies need work. No body is perfect."

Except yours, maybe? "What makes you think I want a job here?"

He sauntered back around the counter, poured the juice in a small glass, and set the drink in front of her. "Karen pointed you out to me. Said you came in for a massage and inquired about a position."

She'd forgotten. "Oh, yes. I was just making small talk."

He picked up a business card and handed it to her. "If you change your mind about that *position*, write down your name and cell number." He winked. "And I'll see what I can arrange."

Heather didn't know how to take that remark. She put her hands on her hips, took a deep breath, and glared at him. Using her 'power pose' had always been effective at the office. He didn't seem to notice it. Or maybe he just needed reminding.

"Your *girlfriend* said you didn't have any *jobs* available right now." She grabbed the glass of juice and took a cautious sip, slightly sweet. cool and refreshing.

His thin lips curved into a sly grin. "That doesn't mean I won't in the near future. I want to start offering classes—Karate, Tai Chi, Qi Gong, Yoga—folks eat that up. And a sophisticated woman like you working for me would draw in a much higher class of people."

How could he afford to expand? Unless he suddenly came into a lot of money. Possibly her aunt's winnings? Or Krystal Stamos agreed to keep the place open and was investing in it. "Sorry, I'm not qualified to teach any of those things."

His grin spread to his eyes. "You wouldn't have to. Just be charming. Engage the customers in some witty conversation and... ya know, make sure your spandex outfit enhances your natural, but toned, curves."

Heather picked up her glass and downed the rest of the drink. "Since I won't be in town long, I'm sorry to say that I'll have to decline your offer. How much do I owe you for the juice?"

"It's on the house."

"Thanks."

She couldn't wait to get back to her room and take a shower to wash this place off.

Chapter 18

HEATHER got in her rental and drove past the off-track betting parlor on the way to the hotel. She recognized Nikos's former accountant, Johnny Tanner, as he walked along the street in front of the building. He turned the corner.

The place is closed. What's he doing there?

Wide-awake and alert, as if she'd chugged a gallon of coffee, Heather had to wonder what Dutch put in that drink. She drove her car around the corner and watched Tanner walk into the alley behind the building. She pulled into a parking space, got out, and followed him.

He's going into the off-track betting parlor. What's up?

She tiptoed toward the back door. Grabbing a tissue from her purse, she rubbed off a circle of grime from the window, and peered inside.

Tanner and Krystal Stamos sat at a document-covered round table that was probably used for card games. Practically head-to-head, they appeared to be reading one of the papers.

Going over her father's finances? Or they might be trying to figure out how to do a grand re-opening in time for the Derby, Saturday. I wish I could see what they're reading.

With her senses heightened from that drink Dutch gave her, she was aware of footsteps approaching. She shoved her hand into her purse and felt around for the pepper spray. With her other hand, she grabbed the door handle in case she needed to go inside for help.

A finger tapped her shoulder. She spun around, and with the pepper spray clutched in her fist, she punched the person in the stomach with all the force she could muster.

"Oooph." A man doubled over. "Why did you do that?" Chad groaned. A moment later, he straightened. "I know you're angry with me for some reason, but punching me was uncalled for."

Embarrassment settled on her shoulders as a dull pain shot through her arm. "I'm sorry. I didn't know who it was." Not that she hadn't thought about doing that ever since she learned about him spying for Jack. She dropped the pepper spray in her purse and grabbed her wrist in an attempt to stop the ache. "Guess I'm a little paranoid from living in the city."

He clutched his stomach. "What are you doing back here, anyway?"

"You should know. You've been following me from the day I arrived." She shook out her hand to get the blood flowing again.

"Why would I want to follow you?"

She opened her mouth to tell him he knew exactly why, when he said, "And don't tell me I know, because I don't." He leaned in close, his lips curving into a disarming smile. "Maybe I do. There's a lot of the siren in you—unconscious, but it's there. I felt it the first time I saw you, sitting at that table in the hotel restaurant with your long auburn hair swept over your shoulder. You almost took my breath away."

His gaze was as soft as a caress. Her stomach fluttered. She lowered her eyelids. "Your feeble attempt at made-up flattery is offensive. Now go away. I'm busy."

"What could you be busy with in this alley?"

"I'm just getting acquainted with your nice little town."

"I hope you're not attempting to investigate Nikos's murder on your own."

She sucked in a breath of frustration. "Why would you think that?"

"You were peering in the back window of the off-track betting parlor. I saw Tanner go in there when I was on my way to the bookstore. And I spotted you getting out of your car and walking the same way."

"Oh, I get it. Once a P.I., always a P.I.?"

"Something like that."

"Well you can tell Jack Steele he can call off his watchdog. Why doesn't he just leave me alone? I've made it abundantly clear I *never* want to see him again."

Chad's forehead furrowed as he glared at her. A moment later, his face relaxed as if an idea struck him. "We're not talking about the same things, are we?"

"I'm talking about the lawyer you're working for."

"And I told you, it would be against the law for me to work as a P.I. without a license."

"Well, it hasn't stopped you from—"

The back door of the building swung open, and Tanner stuck his head out. "What's going on out here?"

They both turned to look at him. Heather had to think of something to get inside. She gathered her courage. "I have an emergency." She bounced up and down on the balls of her feet. "May I please use your bathroom?"

Tanner's thick lips curved into a frown. "I don't know. This ain't my place." He turned his head and called out, "There's a lady here who needs to use the can."

Krystal appeared behind him. She glanced a Heather. "Sure."

He opened the door wider and pointed to a long hallway. "It's right there."

"Thanks." Heather scrunched her nose at Chad and rushed in.

Krystal put a hand on her slim hip. "Well, well. Look who's finally come around. Hi, Chad."

Heather hadn't expected to hear that. She turned as Chad strolled in. "Just getting my new friend acquainted with the neighborhood." His eyes pleaded with her to agree.

You owe me big time. "Yes, acquainted. And now I *really* have to go." She ran toward the bathroom.

Heather came out five minutes later. She glanced around. No one was in the back room. Good. The papers lying across the table had been scooped up into one neat stack and placed face down, with an eight-ball paper weight on top. She pushed the ball aside and fingered through the pile. Corporate spreadsheets.

Tax forms. Easy for her to interpret, she'd done so many.

Evidently, Nikos hadn't paid taxes in years, and he was in debt to the IRS for hundreds of thousands. No wonder he needed Julia's winnings. And he was probably pressuring everyone who owed him. *Now all I have to do is figure out who they are.*

A brushing noise came from the back of the room. Flipping the papers over, she dropped the eight-ball on top, and spun around. A stoop-shouldered man with salt-and-pepper hair, wearing a shabby, gray raincoat pushed a broom. She couldn't take her eyes off him. *Could it possibly be the same guy?* Only one way to find out.

"Excuse me, sir."

"Buddy. They call me Buddy."

She walked up to him. He stopped, put his two work-worn, filthy hands on top of the broom handle, and looked up at her, his tired eyes the same washed out gray as his raincoat.

"Whatsa matter? Ain't I doin' a good enough job?"

"You're doing a great job, Buddy. Do you often take odd jobs around town?"

"When I can get 'em."

"I'd like to ask you a couple of questions, if you don't mind."

He sniffed. "You smell nice. What's that called?"

"Sweat. I came here from the gym."

"On you, it's..." He gave her the O.K. sign with his fingers.

She had to smile. "Thanks. You're the only person who's ever... Well, anyway. Do you remember what you were doing on the night Nikos was killed?"

"I don't know. Time gets away from me."

"It was Friday, three nights ago. Were you working at the hotel?"

He thought a moment. "Sometimes they have jobs for me. Mostly cleanup."

"On this particular night, do you remember dressing up like a waiter and taking a bottle of wine to one of the rooms on the third floor—to a short lady with red hair?"

He scratched his head. "Memory's not too good. I might've."

"Can you tell me who asked you to do that?"

He glanced from side to side as if someone was watching and lowered his voice. "That answer is gonna cost ya."

"I don't have a job right now and not much money. I'll probably be homeless too, very soon. This information could save my aunt from being arrested for a murder she didn't commit."

He placed a finger beside his bulbous nose. "The red-haired lady your aunt?"

"Yes."

He rubbed his whiskered chin and sucked in air through his yellowed teeth. "Tell ya what I'm gonna do. Since I like you, I'll give you a break. One bottle of scotch—the good stuff, single malt. Meet me at the footbridge by the lagoon at ten tonight. And come alone. I don't talk to cops."

This sounded like one of her aunt's old mystery movies. "Couldn't you just give me the name now, and I'll go out and buy you a bottle of scotch?"

He placed a dirt-encrusted finger to his lips. "Shhh. The walls have eyes and ears."

Surveillance? She glanced around. Of course they would have it if they held high-stakes poker games in this room. She hoped it wasn't turned on now. "Fine. I'll be there."

Spiked heels clicked on the floor tiles and echoed through the room. "Buddy, get back to work. And you, stop bothering my janitor."

Krystal, in her slick, black sheath, pushed the eight-ball aside and grabbed the papers from the table.

Who was she calling "you"? Heather worked to keep the calm in her tone. "My name is Heather Stanton."

Krystal uttered a little sound of impatience. "Oh yes, Heather. Chad told me. It just slipped my mind." She gave a one shoulder shrug. "My bad."

My bad? Like that excused her rudeness.

"Thanks for the use of your facilities." Heather flew out the back door and slammed it behind her. A few strides down the alley she stopped. "Chad!"

She'd left him in there. This didn't look good for their cover story. It was too late to go back inside and get him. She'd look ridiculous. Besides, Krystal would take good care of him. They were probably having drinks, talking over old times, and God only knew what else.

She jogged the rest of the way to her car. *Why am I obsessing over this guy? I don't care what they do.*

This was her chance to escape him. She got in her car and put the gearshift in drive. As she checked the street for oncoming traffic, the passenger door opened. Chad slid into the seat and slammed it shut.

"Why did you leave me in there?"

She leaned her head back on the seat rest. "Why does anyone do anything?"

Chad folded his arms. "Stop being obtuse and drive."

"Don't you have your own car?"

"I'll pick it up later."

Heather drove three blocks and turned the corner. She pulled into a parking space in front of the bookstore. "I believe this is where you *get out.*"

Chapter 19

Chad locked the passenger's side door. "Oh no. This is where we finish the conversation we started in the alley."

Heather tightened her grip on the steering wheel and turned to glare at him. Why did he have to be so good-looking?

He softened his gaze. "I don't know what to make of you. One day you're friendly and smiling, and the next..." He lifted his hands in a gesture of frustration. "Would you please clue me in?"

It would feel great to be able to tell him everything. But that wasn't possible, so she'd just clear up one major problem right now.

She took a deep breath to pull her thoughts together. "Fine. I um, looked you up on the internet and found out your last job was as a P.I. for my ex-boyfriend's law firm, Hurst, Rankin, and Steele. Knowing Jack Steele, I'm sure he has you following me, because he's been trying to win me back with pleading phone calls, texts and emails. When that didn't work, flowers and jewelry. Which I returned. It's all been exasperating. So you can tell Jack, no matter what he does, or who he sends to follow me, I'm not going back to him. I refuse to allow that man to take over my life again." She blew out a breath of satisfaction, and leaned back in her seat.

Chad stared at her with an intense look in his eyes. "I see." He unbuckled his seatbelt. "Now you're going to hear my side of the story. But not in the car." He motioned toward the bookstore with his head. "Let's go inside. My sister makes a fresh batch of iced tea every morning. And I'm thirsty."

Heather licked her dry lips. "I suppose I could use something to drink too. And I definitely want to hear what you have to say for yourself."

Chad unlocked the bookstore and invited her in. No sooner had she taken a step inside than Makki jumped on the front counter to greet her with a loud *meow.*

A warm glow spread over Heather. It wasn't often she received unconditional love. She wanted to scoop him up into her arms and kiss his cute little nose. But he wasn't her cat, and she couldn't be sure how he would react. Instead, she said, "Well, hello to you too, sweetheart."

Makki rubbed his face against her hand as she lifted it to stroke the soft fur on his back.

There was something mystical about this place with its beautiful polished oak interior and the smell of old paper, complete with bookstore cat. When the front door closed, the street noises were shut out, and a sense of peace came over her like she'd been absorbed into the store's ambiance.

Tears rose up. She swallowed them back. *What's wrong with me?* Must be all the stress she's under.

"The backroom is this way, remember?" Chad's voice broke into her thoughts. He opened the door, and she walked in.

"You said your sister would be here."

"She's probably in the office doing paperwork. I mean, computer work."

"I thought *this* was your office?"

He glanced at the books lining the shelves. "This is the store room. There's a small office on the other side of the wall. One that actually looks like an office, where Ashley spends Monday mornings going over last week's receipts, paying bills, and filling backorders until we officially open at noon."

She sat in a chair across from his desk. "What's upstairs, more books?"

Chad opened a small refrigerator and took out a large, glass jug. He grabbed two clear glasses from a shelf above it and filled each one with ice and tea. "No, that was our grandfather's apartment. It's vacant now." He closed the fridge.

Heather drank down half the tea. Chad downed his entire glass.

"You really *were* thirsty." Heather put her elbow up on the desk and rested her chin in her hand. "So, when are you going to give Jack my message?"

"First of all, I'm glad you're not seeing him any longer. Was he abusive?"

"Not physically. But after I moved in with him, he turned into a master at gas lighting. For a while he had me believing I was imagining his infidelities, and when I caught him with..." She didn't know the woman's name. "Even then, he tried to explain his way out of it. Lets just say, I'd finally had enough."

Chad's eyes glistened as if he understood. "I know guys like that." He took his empty glass to the small sink. "While it's true I did work for Hurst, Rankin, and Steele, I only stayed a few months, and worked for Henry Rankin, exclusively."

Henry? Her mind made a connection. *Could that possibly be the Henry my aunt Julia had dated for a while?*

"When Rankin passed away—"

"Yes, I remember. Jack didn't like him very much. We did attend his funeral because of the partnership."

"Well, by that time, I'd pretty much had my fill of chasing cheating spouses, and my P.I. license needed to be renewed, so instead of doing that, I decided to come home and help my sister until things got better for her."

Heather took another sip of tea as everything he'd said settled in. "So, what were you doing at the train station on Friday afternoon if you weren't following me?"

"My Aunt Gladys was supposed to come for a visit when she tripped and fell at Union Station before she could get on the train. They sent her to the hospital in an ambulance, where the doctor set her broken ankle, but with everything that happened, she forgot to call me. She didn't contact us until several hours later. I was at the hotel because I thought she'd gotten off the train and went there to meet me. That was our arrangement."

"And so you were following my Aunt Julia, assuming it was her?" *No wonder she didn't trust you.*

"Well, I hadn't seen Aunt Gladys is quite a few years, and the resemblance is uncanny. However, that's where it ends. My aunt has a totally different personality than yours."

Heather could only shake her head at how her perception of things was so far off the mark. "I'm sorry for anything insulting I may have said to you."

"You're forgiven. Friends again?" He put his hand out.

She shook it. "Friends."

"Good." His soft smile spread to his eyes.

A warm, mellow glow washed over her once again. "Since we're friends, are you still willing to help my aunt with this murder investigation?"

"Of course. As long as you're honest with me."

"To tell you the truth, I've learned quite a bit this morning about others who might be suspects. I don't know how to interpret the information."

"Just go to the police. Detective Lindsey needs all the cooperation he can get. As a matter of fact, he's enlisted me as a non-paid consultant on this case. That's how desperate he is."

"I'm not sure I should. I don't want to point a finger at anyone who might be innocent." She finished the ice tea and got up to set her glass in the sink.

"The police will determine that."

Heather checked the time on her cell and pressed her aunt's number. "I'm sure they will, but I don't want to get into it right now. I have to take a shower and change before I go to the station."

"I think you look great."

"Thanks, but I also have to check on my aunt. She's not answering her phone, and I don't trust her. I keep thinking she's going to pack up and run. She tends to do that when she can't cope, and she's got this crazy idea our family is related to people in the mafia, and they'll make her magically disappear so the police will never find her."

"Sounds like something my Aunt Gladys would say."

"Really?"

Chad shook his head. "No, not at all. I just wanted you to lighten up."

Heather couldn't stop herself from smiling. "Thanks."

"Before you go, let's exchange cell numbers so we can keep in touch just in case something comes up and I have to contact you or vice versa."

Afterward, Heather scooted out the door of the bookstore and rushed to her car. *Please let Aunt Julia be at the hotel.*

Chapter 20

HEATHER pulled into the hotel parking lot and ran to the entrance.

As she passed the front desk, the clerk said, "More flowers came for you."

Probably from Jack. She got in the elevator and stuck her head out. "Send them back. Thank you." She pressed the button for the third floor. *Please be there. Please be there.* She ran to her room, pushed the key card in the door, and held her breath as she opened it.

Fresh, colorful flowers greeted her from every corner of the room. It was filled with assorted colors of roses, carnations, mums, and lilies in small vases to gigantic floor arrangements. Aunt Julia sat in the desk chair, her cell phone plugged into the wall.

"It's about time you got back. I feel like I'm at my own funeral for cripes sake. I like flowers, but this..." She spread her arms out. The expression on her aunt's face was somewhere between disbelief and horror.

Heather gasped. "Does Jack think he can win me back by overwhelming me with flowers?" She pressed her lips in a tight grimace. "I've forgiven him in the past, but never again."

"Maybe they're not from Jack." Julia handed her a small envelope. "Read this before you jump to conclusions."

Heather took the card out. "Thanks for dinner. Derek." She dropped her tense shoulders and relaxed her expression. "Oh, well that's different. Actually, it's kind of a thoughtful gesture. A little on the overwhelming side, but sweet nonetheless."

"You went on a dinner date while I was rotting in jail?"

What a drama queen. "Oh, Aunt Julia, you weren't rotting. And it wasn't really a date, more like a fact-finding mission. And believe me, I learned a lot."

Julia scrunched her eyes in a look of suspicion. "Then what did you do *after* dinner to warrant all *this*?"

"Nothing. I drove back here, alone, and had a nice chat with Christine Talan. I drank a small brandy in the bar, came back up here, and got into bed. Around midnight I got up to get some water and heard squeaking noises outside our door, like someone was pacing back and forth in the hall. When I looked out the door a while later, I saw the shadow of a man rounding the corner by the elevators. I didn't think there was a man registered on this floor."

"Maybe he was visiting one of the ladies in the other room?" Julia raised her eyebrows.

Heather picked up the hotel phone and pressed the button for the front desk. "Hi, it's Heather Stanton. Could you please tell me if there are any men registered at the hotel who have a room on the third floor?"

"Just a moment." A few keys clicked, and the clerk came back to the phone. "No one's on the third floor, except you and your aunt."

"How about the ladies down the hall?"

"They checked out Sunday afternoon."

"I saw a man up here late last night, around midnight."

"Might have been the janitor. He works at all hours. While I have you on the phone, do you still want me to send those flowers back to the florist?"

"No, but you might find out if there are any places in town where we could donate them."

"I'll see what I can do. Is there anything else I can help you with?"

"No. Thank you." Heather hung up the phone. "The clerk said it was probably the janitor." A little voice at the back of her mind whispered doubt. She scurried to the small closet and grabbed some clean clothes. "I hope this hotel has a laundry."

"Most hotels do." Julia lifted a vase of roses from the desk and looked for a place to move it. "That does it! These are all going out in the hall. The smell is killing my sinuses."

Heather slid open a window for air. "Aunt Julia, when I get out of the shower, we need to have a *serious* talk."

Julia opened the door and rolled the desk chair against it. "By the time you shower and change, these will all be out of here."

Heather headed toward the bathroom. "Did you hear what I said about having a talk?"

"Yeah, I heard. But I have to tell you, I hate the word *serious*."

The hotel phone rang.

Heather turned with a start. "Would you please answer that? If it's Derek, I'm not here."

"Why? Don't you like him?"

She didn't know how she felt about the guy. "We may not be here long, so I'm not interested in getting involved with anyone."

Julia lifted the receiver. "Hello." Long pause, her gaze moving from left to right and back again as she listened. She put a hand over the mouthpiece. "It's for me."

Heather had to wonder who would be calling her aunt on the hotel phone instead of her cell. She showered, dressed, and came out with the blow dryer in her hand.

Julia walked toward the hall holding the last vase of flowers and had to sidestep Derek, who was standing in the open doorway. "Excuse me," she said.

He moved aside and knocked on the frame.

He couldn't have come at a worse time. I must look terrible with no makeup and my hair all wet. "This is a surprise."

"Hi. I see you got my flowers."

"Yes, thanks. It was very sweet of you. One bouquet would have been more than enough."

Seeming to ignore what she said, he gave the grouping a quick glance. "I wanted to make an impression. But why are you moving them to the hallway?"

She didn't want to offend him. He seemed like such a nice guy. "You did make an impression. The smell was overwhelming, so we put them in the hall for a little while to um, get some fresh air in the room. Right, Aunt Julia?"

"Yeah, right. Air." Julia put the vase of roses she carried on the hall floor.

Heather attempted to ease her embarrassment. "We'll bring them in later."

"Not if I can help it," Julia mumbled under her breath as she sauntered back into the room.

Heather ran her fingers through her damp hair. "Sorry, you'll have to excuse my appearance. I wasn't expecting visitors. Why didn't you call?"

Derek took a few more steps in. "I tried. Your hotel line was busy. And I don't have your cell number."

I hope he's not hinting around for it. "So, what brings you here? I thought you worked in the mayor's office on weekdays."

"I do. I'm on lunch."

I'll bet he takes more than an hour.

He gave her his dazzling, white smile. "The reason I came is because I had such a great time at dinner last night, I thought we could do it again tonight. And this time, actually go to a movie afterward."

"I feel bad about the way I left you at the restaurant. I had a lot on my mind."

"I can well imagine. So, how about tonight?"

Chad's face came to mind. "Sorry to disappoint you, but my aunt and I have plans."

"Then why don't you let me take you both to lunch right now?"

While it would have been nice, she needed to talk to Lindsey. "No can do. We're meeting Detective Lindsey at the station house in a little while to discuss a few things... about the murder."

Julia raised both eyebrows and mouthed the word, "What?"

Heather checked the clock radio on the night stand. "We have to be going or we'll be late." She sprinted to the open door and nudged the chair away. "It was generous of you to send all these flowers, and... and everything."

Derek raised an eyebrow and set his lips into a firm line. He wasn't the kind of guy who was deterred easily. "I'll call you."

Heather gave a quick nod as he strolled toward the door. She closed it behind him.

Julia checked her face in the dresser mirror and patted a few loose hairs into place. "What do you mean, we're meeting Detective Lindsey at the station house? You could have let Derek take us to lunch first. I'm starving."

"Let me dry my hair. Then we can go."

***

As Heather pulled her rental car into the police parking lot, Julia scrunched her nose. "Why are we stopping here? You said we were going to lunch."

"We are. Frst I have to tell Detective Lindsey a couple of things I discovered this morning that may help keep you from being arrested for murder."

Julia grabbed the door handle. "I'm all for that."

"Wait! Before we do. I need to ask you one question."

"Shoot." Julia covered her lips. "Bad word choice."

"Is the Henry you told me you were dating, Henry Rankin, one of Jack's partners in the law firm?"

"As a matter of fact, it was. Such an attractive man, and what a horseplayer. We went to the Arlington Park Race Track every weekend. And when he won, he bought me the most gorgeous jewelry."

"Did you know he was married?"

"Divorced."

"No, Aunt Julia. He was married with two grown children. His son is a couple of years older than I am, and his daughter, a few years younger."

Julia's face stiffened as though someone had just struck her. "I can't believe that. Why would he lie?" It softened a bit. "But it just goes to prove what I've been telling you all along. You can't trust men."

"Makes me wonder if his wife or his children knew about you. It would give either of them a motive to frame you for murder."

"Even if they knew who I was, how would they know where I am? And I told you, I had nothing to do with Henry's overdose."

"That might not be the way they see it."

Chapter 21

HEATHER opened the door to the station, and Julia followed her in. Officer Henderson manned the front desk. His brown eyes flashed when he spotted Julia. "What can I do for you?"

Heather gave him a warm smile. "I'd like to talk to Detective Lindsey, please."

"Sorry, he isn't in right now. I'll be glad to take your information and let him know you're looking for him."

He handed her a slip of paper. She wrote down her name and number and handed it back to the officer. "Please tell him it's important. Thanks."

As they walked out the door, Julia said, "That was a waste of time. Can we have lunch now? I'm famished."

"Sure. I know a place in the neighborhood." Heather entered the name in the GPS on her dashboard and waited. "And it's just around the corner."

***

Heather pulled into a parking space near The Club Car Diner.

Julia stared out the front windshield. "This is nothing more than a hot dog stand with a fancy awning. What made you want to come here?"

"Derek mentioned it to me yesterday evening. The name sounded interesting, so I thought we'd give it a try."

Julia stepped out of the car. "I'm ravenous, so why not?"

Heather locked the car and met her aunt at the counter.

"Best burgers and dogs in town," the elderly man in the soiled white apron said. "What'll you have?"

Julia tapped a finger on her lip as she scanned the menu. "A Maxwell Street Polish."

It had been a long time since Heather had eaten one of those. Her dad occasionally brought them home for dinner, before the divorce. She probably shouldn't indulge in all the fat and calories, but it wasn't as if she ate them all the time.

"I'll have the same."

The server winked. "Good choice. Coming right up."

It didn't take long before they picked up their orders. Julia grabbed her lunch and glanced around. "Where do you want to eat?"

The server scooped up the money Heather had placed on the counter. "There are tables around the back."

Six picnic tables in two uneven rows stood on the small paved area behind the stand. Heather spotted a familiar face and walked toward his table.

Julia groaned. "Do we have to eat with *him*?"

"Yes."

She glanced at Heather. "How do I look?"

"You look fine. It's not as if you're meeting him for a date. This is business."

Heather sat across from Detective Lindsey. "Hi. I was just looking for you."

The detective glanced up and wiped his lips with a paper napkin. He turned as Julia slid in next to him "My sergeant notified me you'd been in. I was coming over to see you a little later." He leaned forward, his focus on Heather. "What do you want to talk to me about?"

She set the paper wrapper with her lunch on the table. "When I was working out at Dutch's gym this morning, he told me he's thinking of expanding and offered me a job. But Saturday, when I was at the day spa, I heard he was broke. Where would he get the money to do that?"

"He could be using the money that's owed to me," Julia suggested. "He probably stole the winning ticket from Nikos after he killed him and is waiting until everything calms down to cash it in."

The detective crushed the paper bag he held. "Don't go throwing accusations around. We can't arrest anyone on conjecture. We need evidence. And there isn't one bit of evidence linking Dutch to the murder."

There has to be something. "Isn't the fact there's no evidence, in itself evidence?"

"Don't try to double-talk me, Miss Stanton. The laws are clearly laid out."

"Maybe you don't have to follow the laws completely," Julia pleaded. "Maybe there's some bending room?"

Lindsey's eyes sparked with anger. "There's no bending room! Circumstance and speculation will never trump fact. And the fact is that Dutch has a rock-solid alibi." He rubbed his forehead. "And I know where he's getting the money to expand. It's perfectly legitimate."

Heather digested this information for a few moments. *Maybe Nikos left him his half of the business.* "What other leads do you have? There should be other suspects. What about Buddy?"

"We're looking for him. I still think it's odd no one at the hotel or in the bar that night saw this guy who allegedly brought your aunt a bottle of wine, except your aunt."

Someone must be lying. "Derek Kane said he sold a man a bottle of wine at the bar."

"He also said he does that all the time, so it didn't seem unusual. And he didn't remember the guy's face."

"Well, I think it was Buddy," Heather said. "And I can tell you where he is right now."

The detective put his elbows on the table and clasped his hands together. "How would you know where he is?"

"I came across a man who looked very much like the one my aunt described. He was sweeping out Nikos's place just thirty minutes ago. He said his name was Buddy."

The detective glared at her. "From what I understand, it's closed. How did you get in there?"

"I was in the area, and I needed to use the bathroom. Krystal let me in. And on the way out, I talked with Buddy myself. He practically admitted to taking the wine up to my aunt's room. When I questioned him about who asked him to do that, he couldn't say because 'the walls have ears'. I think he meant the place has surveillance. So we set up a meeting in the park at ten tonight. He said he'd tell me then."

"We'll keep looking for him. Don't even think about meeting this guy. If he's an accomplice to murder, it could be dangerous."

"Even if you do find him, he said he won't talk to the cops. I have a better chance of finding out who he was working for if I meet him alone."

"I can't tell you what to do, Miss Stanton, so I'm giving you a little advice. Don't meet with this man. But on the other hand, if *you're* the accomplice to a murder, maybe I should be warning *him* about you."

Heather narrowed her eyes. This must be part of his technique, trying to make her angry so she'd talk without thinking. She bit back the first caustic response that came to mind and made an effort to control the emotion in her voice.

"I also found out Nikos hadn't paid his income taxes in years, and he owed thousands to the IRS. It might be why he needed my aunt's winnings. And he may have been pressuring or blackmailing everyone who owed him money." She gave the detective a sharp nod to make a point. "You might look into who those people are, too."

As he listened, his expression—at first condescending, became non-committal, then speculative. Evidently nothing surprised him. "We're in the process of investigating that. His accountant came forward with the information about the taxes Nikos owed, yesterday."

Heather picked up her lunch. "If he was duplicitous in tax evasion, then you might look into the accountant's finances also. I hear he's a horseplayer. Maybe he was siphoning the tax money into a private account to use for gambling, and Nikos found out about it."

"He might be a very creative accountant," Julia added.

The detective raised an eyebrow. "You've been very busy." He grunted. "So have I. This morning I learned that the gun in the Willowses' backyard is registered to a Mr. Stanley Fairchild." He looked at Julia. "Your ex-husband. And Mr. Fairchild said he gave it to you as a gift."

Julia stop chewing and swallowed. Her eyes scanned the area around the table as she dabbed at her lips with a napkin. "Yes, Stan gave me a gun."

Detective Lindsey narrowed his eyes. "So, you admit the derringer is *your* gun?"

"All I'm saying is the gun is mine. That doesn't prove I killed Nikos with it."

"Several patrons at the off-track betting parlor and in the hotel bar, said they saw you two having a heated argument."

"Just because I argued with him, doesn't necessarily mean I killed him. And if you think I did, well, you'll just have to prove it."

Lindsey's eyes bulged, and his mouth fell open. His top lip curved into a one-sided grin. "You're wrong. That's the district attorney's job. Mine is to gather evidence. And when the reports come back from ballistics and fingerprinting, I'll have it." He leaned forward, his gaze steady on Julia. "And then I can make an arrest."

These weren't simple statements, they had force behind them, like revolver shots.

He jumped to his feet, stepped over the bench, and tossed his crushed paper bag into a nearby trash container. "Just a reminder. Don't leave town. And don't do anything stupid."

As he walked away, Julia's worried eyes followed him to his car. She crumpled the paper from her lunch in her trembling hands. "I told you that man is out to get me." She had that scared rabbit look again as she grabbed a tiny mint from her purse and popped it into her mouth. "So, what do I do now, sit around and wait for him to arrest me? I can't go back to that jail cell—I won't!"

Heather stressed over what to say to comfort her aunt. The right words forever alluded her. And the wrong words made her sound heartless and uncaring. It's probably where she got the reputation for being cold. Her sister, Emily, was the sympathetic one. She always knew the right thing to say. *Too bad she isn't here now.*

No matter how Heather felt about her aunt at the moment, she couldn't waste time on sympathy and emotionalism. She had to take a firm stand for Julia's own good.

"I know things seem hopeless right now, but we can face whatever comes, as long as we stick together. Don't even *think* about running away."

"Who's running away?" A man's voice cut into their conversation.

Heather turned and glanced up at the guy standing behind her. "Oh, hello."

Derek gave them both his charming smile. "If I knew you were coming here, I would have bought your lunches. It's a great place to grab a burger. I thought you were meeting Detective Lindsey at the station for a talk?"

Heather turned to meet Julia's gaze. "We did go there to talk to him, but he wasn't there. He was here."

Julia popped another mint into her mouth. "He said once he gets all the evidence together, he's making an arrest, and from the look in his eyes, I think he means me."

Derek seated himself next to Julia. "So that's why you're thinking of running away. I can't blame you. After all, several people saw you pull out that derringer and put it on the bar at Nikos's place Friday evening. That's pretty intimidating."

"Then you must have heard him goad me into doing it." Julia dropped the mints in her purse.

Derek's full lips turned into a scowl. "Yeah, he sure knew how to push people's buttons." Then the scowl turned into a smile. "Running would be an exciting, romantic adventure, with a brawny cop on your heels chasing you around the country. Kind of like the female version of *The Fugitive*."

Heather put her hand up to stop him from saying any more. "Don't encourage her."

"Who me? Far from it." Derek took a business card from his pocket and handed it to Julia. He winked. "Call me if you need anything. Anything at all."

Julia gave a curt nod, grabbed the card, and slipped in into her purse. "Now there's a man who understands me."

No. There's a man who can spot a vulnerable woman a mile away. Heather couldn't wait to leave before he said any more to egg her aunt on.

"Aunt Julia and I have a lot of things to do this afternoon, so if you'll excuse us, we really have to be going." She stood and tossed what was left of her lunch in the trash.

Julia grinned at Derek. "Nice seeing you again."

Heather smiled her goodbye. She gripped her aunt's arm, and led her to the car.

First, he tried to charm her, and now he was getting to her aunt. Some guys just didn't know when to quit.

Julia patted Heather's shoulder. "I hope you don't think I took what Derek said about running away, seriously. Don't worry about me. I promise not to run this time. And my word is my bond. As long as I have you on my side, I know I can make it through all this."

Heather unlocked the car doors. "That's right. Together we're strong, and we can do anything." *Well, almost anything.*

Julia was silent a moment, as if she was thinking everything over. "If Detective Lindsey needs evidence, we'll have to find him some." She slipped into the passenger's seat. "So, how do we do that?"

Heather went around the back and got in the driver's side. "I don't have a clue. But I have a feeling it involves doing something stupid."

Chapter 22

JULIA snapped her fingers. "I've just had an epiphany."

This should be good. "I don't have any ideas, so let's hear it."

"I need to go to the pawnshop and see if I can find something that might help us with our investigation."

Heather turned the steering wheel to round the corner. "What do you think you're going to find there?"

"I'll go, I'll see. First, I want to stop off at the hotel and pick up my red stiletto sandals. Maybe the pawn broker will give me a few bucks for them since they're brand new. Well, only worn once for a couple hours."

"You just got money when you pawned your jewelry, Saturday."

Julia opened her large purse and rummaged around inside. "Most of that's gone."

"Where could you possibly have spent it?" Heather had been buying all their meals.

Julia pulled out her wallet and checked inside. "While you were away this morning, I paid some of my bills at the Currency Exchange, and I bought a few essentials at the drug store."

Heather had wondered why her aunt was already dressed when she got back. She finally pulled into the hotel parking lot. "Okay, but I've got bills to pay, too." *Before my money runs out.* And I have some computer work to do, so we'll have to make it a quick stop."

***

By five o'clock, Heather's eyes hurt from staring at the computer screen for hours, paying bills, reading and answering emails, and checking for job opportunities. Not to mention the personal snooping. She closed her laptop, convinced there was nothing left to discover.

"There's only so much information on Nikos, Krystal, and the other people involved in this murder case that I can find, legally. What we need is someone who has access to websites that I don't."

Aunt Julia, looking despondent at spending the afternoon watching old movies and chomping on mint after mint while waiting for a knock on the door from the police, jumped out of her chair. "No. What we need is someone who knows everyone and everything that goes on in this town. Let's try the desk clerk, she might know someone who could help us."

Heather gathered her previously worn clothes. She shoved them into a plastic bag the hotel had provided. "Let's take our things down and find out where laundry facilities are. I'd also like to find out what progress she's made on getting rid of those flowers in the hall."

After Julia gathered her things, they went down to the front desk. The name on the slender, twenty-something clerk's tag read *Vikki Garrett.* Her pale brown eyes moved from the computer screen to Heather's face. "Can I help you?"

Heather held up her clothes bag. "Where are the guest laundry facilities?"

The clerk pushed a lock of dark, curly hair from her forehead. "We have a dry cleaning service that will pick up your things. If you want to wash them yourselves, there's a small laundry room with coin-operated machines down the hallway, next to the side entrance."

"There's a side entrance?" *Was that how the murderer got in and out without anyone noticing?*

"Yes. There's also a kitchen entrance around the back."

"I know about the kitchen entrance, we've used it. I didn't know you had a side door."

"It's pretty out of the way. I keep telling the hotel manager he needs to put a camera there, so we can see who's coming and going. And now with this murder, I've been locking it."

"Did you work the night shift last Friday when the murder happened?"

Vikki's curls bounced as she moved her head to look at the computer screen. "I switched shifts with Christine that night. She came in around seven the next morning. The clerk's voice was thick and unsteady. "And I can tell you, I was sorry I did. I'll never do that again."

"So I'm assuming you've already told the police you didn't see anyone suspicious. Who else was working at the hotel that night?"

The clerk's head jerked up as her gaze probed the ceiling in thought. "Just the usual people." She looked at Heather. "And our part-time janitor. He must have come to pick up his pay packet, because he wasn't supposed to be here that night."

Heather crossed her fingers. "What time was that?"

The clerk rubbed her chin. "It may have been around ten or so."

Heather exchanged glances with her aunt and set her clothes bag down. "Is your part-time janitor a homeless man, salt-and-pepper hair, stooped shoulders, wears an old gray rain coat, goes by the name of Buddy?"

The clerk's eyes flashed in recognition. "Yeah, that's him. Buddy Maruzy."

"Do you have any idea where he hangs out?"

"Why are you interested in him?"

How do I explain this? "If he's truly homeless, I might be able to help him."

"All I know is, he gave the address of an abandoned store front. The one next door to the Salvation Army Center on Bleaker Street."

"Thanks for the information." Heather picked up her bag and pulled her aunt aside. "I wonder if Buddy could have borrowed a waiter's jacket, slipped it on, cleaned up a bit, and brought you the wine. Did you notice if he smelled or if his hands were dirty?"

Julia scrunched her nose. "I didn't notice either of those things. I mean, I was furious at Nikos, and I didn't get close enough to the guy to smell him or to see his hands. Although, after he left, I did think the room needed airing."

"Did you tip him?"

"Actually, no. He wasn't around long enough. I thought it was unusual. The man was in and out of my room in a flash. Come to think of it, I'm pretty sure I didn't slip the security latch on the door, either."

"That tells me a lot." Heather started toward the laundry room. "Let's each put a load of wash in and get some dinner. I'm going to meet this guy at the park at ten. He promised to tell me who hired him. Then I'll report it to the police. I'm pretty sure Detective Lindsey won't arrest you once he gets this information, even if your fingerprints *are* on the gun." *Which they undoubtedly will be.*

After loading the two washing machines, Heather and her aunt passed through the lobby on their way to the restaurant. Heather caught sight of a table with colorful carnations and approached the clerk again.

"I forgot to ask you, have you made any progress with getting my flowers distributed?"

"A little. The hospital will take some tomorrow. They're sending a driver to pick them up in the morning. And The Willow Tree Retirement Village is willing to take a few if we can bring them over, except we don't have anyone to do that right now."

Heather had hours to kill before her meeting with Buddy tonight. "My aunt and I aren't doing anything after dinner, except laundry. We'd be happy to take them."

The clerk's eyes twinkled. "Great. I think there are some empty boxes in the kitchen you can use to secure the flowers for transport. I'll let the director know you're coming and ask how many she wants."

***

After dinner, Heather, Julia, and two kitchen staff packed up the six vases of flowers in the boxes provided, and loaded them into Heather's rental. She drove to the retirement village where the grateful staff accepted the flowers.

On the way back, Heather stopped at the supermarket to pick up a bottle of scotch for Buddy and a six-pack of spring water for herself and Julia.

In their hotel room, Heather opened her laptop and Googled the Illinois Property Owners Search website to find out who owned the storefront where Buddy probably lived, but she couldn't remember any of the building numbers on Bleaker Street. So she entered the information for the Salvation Army Store and the buildings next to it.

Julia turned on the television. She picked up a bottle of water and the bottle of scotch. "I'm glad you bought this. The drinks at this hotel are so expensive."

"No! Put that down." Heather shot to her feet. "I didn't buy it for us. It's my bribe for Buddy."

Julia's hand jittered and flipped her cup over as she set the bottle back on the desk, the water splashing on the label.

"Now, look what you made me do." Julia picked it up. "The label's soaked." She ran to the bathroom, and came out rubbing it with a hand towel.

Heather grabbed the towel from her aunt and sopped up the water on the desk. Julia passed her the bottle, and Heather tore off a small part of the label that had come loose. "It's okay, I don't think he'll mind if it's not perfect."

She picked up the laptop to check the screen. The results showed, The Willows Investment Group. Chadwick Emerson Willows II, CEO.

Chad owned it? *Oh wait, he's the third. Must be his dad.* Heather glanced at the time on her laptop and turned it off. "I've got to get going if I want to meet Buddy at ten."

Julia turned the volume down on the television. "Are you sure you want to do this?" Her eyebrows scrunched. "Maybe it would be safer if I came with you."

"He specifically told me to come alone. I'll call you when I get to the park, and we'll keep the phone lines open. If you hear anything suspicious, call the police on the hotel phone." Heather picked up her purse and flung the strap over her shoulder. She patted the side. "And remember, I've got my trusty pepper spray. It shoots from six feet away."

"That won't do any good if the man's behind you." Julia flicked off the television. "I can't let you do this alone. I insist on going with you. I'd feel a lot more confident if I had my gun, but since I don't..." She grabbed her purse and pulled out a small pair of binoculars, a little larger than opera glasses.

"I didn't know you had those." Heather picked up the scotch bottle and shoved it in the crook of her arm.

"I traded my stilettos for them at the pawnshop. They come in handy at the track. But *these* are special. They're digital camera binoculars. You can take pictures with them—you know, for when the horses finish nose-to-nose."

Aunt Julia said it with such confidence, Heather had to wonder if she intended to use them at the races soon. "I thought you needed cash?"

"I do, and I'll get it when I no longer have a use for these. I can pawn them again." Julia slipped the binocular strap around her neck. "I'll watch you from the car, and if I see that guy lay one hand on you, I'll come running."

Is she kidding? "And do what?"

Julia stepped into her sneakers. "Don't you worry about that." She stooped down and pulled a yellow, plastic baseball bat from under her bed. "I got *this* at the drugstore this morning."

Oh, my God! "I hope you don't intend to use it."

"Only if I need to." Julia held her hand up and crossed her fingers. "This is for luck, 'cause we're gonna need it."

Chapter 23

HEATHER pulled her rental car up to the curb across the street from the park and glanced at her aunt. She took a deep breath to strengthen her bravado as she pointed to the bench by the bridge over the lagoon. "I'll be right there."

Julia gazed through the binoculars. "I see it. And don't worry, I'll have an eye on you every minute and an ear on my cell phone."

Heather fused her courage with determination and stepped out of the Chevy. A warm breeze stirred the willow branches, filling the park with whisperings, even though no one else was around. As she made her way to the bridge, her shoes scrunched on the gravel path, and twigs snapped under her feet. She surrendered to the urge to glance over her shoulder... more than once.

Finally reaching the stone structure, she called her aunt's cell. "I'm here."

"I can see you, no thanks to those park lights. They're really dim."

"Just don't hang up. And keep it on mute unless you absolutely have to get my attention."

Heather shoved her phone in her jeans pocket. She ran her thumb nail across her bottom lip as she glanced at the fireflies dancing above the water. The old-fashioned lights *were* dim. And far between. But the moon —large, bright, and full—cast its light across the still shadows in the park.

The bell in the church tower doled ten times.

After that, everything went quiet.

Then, something moved.

Every nerve in Heather's body tensed. Instinct from years of living in the city cautioned her to turn around. A weighted, paper grocery bag blindsided her. She stumbled sideways. Her knees buckled as her body tumbled to the wet grass by the lagoon. The liquor bottle was snatched from her grasp.

In the space of a heartbeat, everything was quiet again. She dragged herself up and glanced around. A cloaked figure melted like a shadow into the darkness.

The incongruous sound of a car broke through the night, squealing up to the bridge, the headlights blinding her.

She shaded her eyes and reached for her purse to grab the pepper spray. Her purse wasn't there. Panic scorched her insides. It must have fallen off near the bridge somewhere. She dropped to her knees and scrambled to search the area.

A car door opened and slammed shut. Her heart beat to near suffocation. She tensed, ready for a fight, or the fastest sprint of her life.

Julia came out of the car, wielding the baseball bat. She took off through the trees after the man. Heather struggled for breath as relief washed over her. She ran a few feet up the bridge and used the flashlight on her cell to see if she could spot where her aunt had gone before following her.

A few moments later, Julia sauntered out of the trees, swinging Heather's purse. "He saw me coming and dropped it."

The situation was so bizarre, Heather let out a light laugh. She wasn't sure if it was from relief that her aunt was okay or from the smug look on Julia's face as she swung the purse in one hand and the bat in the other.

"That was a crazy thing to do, Aunt Julia. You could have been hurt or killed."

Julia handed her the purse and put a comforting hand on Heather's shoulder. "Don't worry about me. I can take care of myself. I've had to for a long time. I got your purse back, but I'm sorry to say, he got away with the booze."

"I don't care about that. I'm only glad you're okay." Heather glanced at the car. "You weren't supposed to drive across the grass."

"They do things like that in the movies all the time. Indiana Jones drove through a college library on a motorcycle." She popped a mint into her mouth.

"That was his son."

"Six of one..."

Her aunt was impossible. "Yes, but this isn't the movies."

At the foot of the bridge, a man walked around Heather's car, inspecting the inside. She tensed again. *I hope it's not the police.* Aunt Julia didn't need anything else on her record.

"Is anyone hurt?" Chad's voice cut through her fear.

She let out a breath to release the tension as her spirits lightened. "No, we're fine."

His hand rushed to his chest. "Thank goodness. I thought you might have been in an accident."

Julia hid the bat behind her back. "We weren't."

"Then why is your car sitting here at such an odd angle?" He looked from one to the other for an answer. When neither said anything, he offered, "May I suggest you get it back on the street before the cops spot it and have it towed away?"

Julia tsked. "I'll do it." She moved near Heather and whispered, "I'll be waiting for you on the other side of the street."

Before Heather could stop her, Julia dashed into the car and drove across the grass again. Heather turned to Chad, who seemed unaffected by her aunt's actions. He might not have realized Julia's driver's license had been confiscated.

Heather hugged her arms to her chest. "I can't say I'm not glad to see you, but what are you doing in the park at this time of night? Don't tell me you were taking a shortcut home again."

"Detective Lindsey sent me. You told him the time you'd be at the park to meet Buddy but not the location. I've been walking around looking for you. No use asking why you went off without telling me," Chad growled. "You think you're too smart to need help?"

Under his questioning gaze, she looked up into his warm eyes, and something strange happened. One moment she was conscious of the dim park lights and the willow branches fluttering in the night breeze. Of a frog splashing on his lily pad and crickets chirping.

Chad's dark head bent toward her, and suddenly she was so acutely aware of the man himself that everything else became unreal, like something in a dream.

When she didn't answer, Chad's eyebrows lowered in a concerned look. "Something wrong?"

She stared at his handsome face, now illuminated only by the lamplight. Without taking her eyes from him, she moved her head from side to side in slow motion. "No. I um..."

"Well, did you meet with Buddy?"

His words broke the spell, bringing her thoughts back to the conversation. "Unfortunately, a man came along, wacked me with a loaded shopping bag, and stole my purse, and the bottle of scotch. It must've been him. Who else knew I'd be here?"

"A bottle of scotch?"

"My bribe."

"You've got to report this to the police."

"And have Detective Lindsey know I came to the park after he warned me not to?" She wasn't looking forward to a lecture from him.

Chad pointed to the handbag she had clutched to her chest. "Looks like you still have your purse."

"My aunt got it back."

"Your aunt?" His voice was curt. "That was a very foolish thing to do. She could have been killed, and for what? A handbag that's only worth a few dollars."

"Try five hundred."

Chad shook his head. "I'll never understand women and their need for expensive accessories. I hate to play Devil's advocate, but have you looked inside?"

The zipper was undone, so she checked. "No wonder he was so eager to let my aunt have it back. My wallet's gone." She put a hand to her forehead. "This is just great!" Then her brain sparked an idea. "Maybe he just took the money out and threw the wallet away." She pulled out her phone and turned on the flashlight app again.

Chad took his phone out and did the same. They searched the ground around the bridge and in the direction the man ran, but found nothing.

Heather glanced at the water, glistening under the lamplight. "Maybe he threw it in the lagoon."

"If it hasn't sunk, you'd be able to see it floating on top. I don't think you'd want to go in and look for it, the water's pretty deep. It grades down to about twelve feet in the middle. My friends and I used to fish here when we were kids. It's icy cold, a half block wide, and two blocks long." He glanced at the dark clouds now covering the moon. "And from the rumble of thunder I just heard, I think it's going to rain soon."

Would it be worth trudging into the water to search for her wallet? As she stood frozen to the spot, studying the murky lagoon, a vigorous wind whipped the willow branches into a frenzy. Huge swirls of dirt and debris flew up from every direction, encircling them like a whirlwind. A streak of lightning flashed across the sky. Heather shut her eyes and cringed.

Chad flung his arms around her. She snuggled her face into his shoulder, absorbing the scent of his musky aftershave, the freshly laundered shirt, the warmth of his touch. She gave in to the reassuring feel of his hands on her back, enjoying the closeness.

He put his lips to her ear and murmured, "Let's get out of here."

Chad kept his arm around her shoulders as they made their way to his car a split-second before the torrential rain.

Brushing back her tangle of auburn hair, Heather stared at the streams of water washing across the front windshield. "Well, there goes any evidence of my assault." She leaned her head against the seat in defeat. "And my wallet."

Remembering her aunt, she frantically searched for her cell number and called. "Hello, are you okay?"

"I'm tired of sitting here in this storm. Where the heck are you?"

"I'm in Chad's car."

"Good, then he can drive you back to the hotel, which is where I'm going just as soon as this rain calms down."

"But you don't have a..." Julia cut off the call before Heather could say the words *driver's license.*

Then again, neither do I.

The rain let up soon after it had started, so Chad drove them to the police station. On the way, Heather told him everything she'd said to the detective earlier.

The officer on duty took the details of her assault. Afterward, he gave her all the information she needed to file a stolen driver's license report and cancel her credit cards.

"Can you send a policeman to the empty storefront on Bleaker Street where Buddy hangs out to see if you can get my wallet back, in case he was the one who stole it?" she asked the officer.

Busy typing in her information into the computer, he said, "Sorry, lightning struck one of the power lines on the north side of town. We need all the officers and Emergency Services Volunteers to man the streets there."

She turned to Chad. "What am I going to do with no ATM card, no credit cards, and no driver's license? I have to drive my aunt to the police station for her community service in the morning."

"I can instruct someone to pick her up," the officer said.

Heather stood. "Thanks. Are we finished?"

"Sure. You're free to go anytime."

Chad was already on his feet as she rose from her chair. They walked out the door together. "I'll drive you to the DMV to get another copy of your driver's license. They should have the police report on file by morning."

In the parking lot, Heather stopped walking and looked up at him. "I just thought of something else. I don't have identification with me. I think I'll have to go to city hall, or contact the Office of Vital Records, to get a copy of my birth certificate before we go to the DMV."

"I'll take you to City Hall, and we'll see what they have to say."

Heather was grateful she had someone to help, but there was still that urgency to retrieve her stolen things. She might not have to go through the hassle of replacing everything tomorrow if Chad would cooperate tonight.

"I've just had an idea. Why don't *we* go to that storefront on Bleaker Street and see if Buddy left my wallet there? Maybe he only wanted the cash, which wasn't much, so I don't care about that. I won't press charges if I can find everything else."

Chad's gaze searched her eyes. "Are you sure you want to do that? If we're caught, it's breaking and entering."

Didn't he know? "You should be able to go in with no problem. After all, your dad owns the building."

His mouth curved into an unconscious smile. "My dad owns it?"

She took out her cell phone and scrolled to the Illinois Property Owners Search website. "It says here that the building belongs to The Willows Investment Group. Chadwick Emerson Willows II, CEO. Isn't that your dad?"

"It is." Chad's jaw dropped open. "That was very enterprising of you. I'd forgotten that group of stores was part of my dad's old investment property." He motioned toward the car with his head. "Let's go."

Chad drove to Bleaker Street where he parked in front of the Salvation Army store. "We don't want Buddy to see us approach in case he's in there." His arm brushed her legs as he opened the glove compartment to grab a large flashlight. "Sorry."

Her face flushed, and she was thankful he couldn't see in the dark. "It's okay."

Most of the street lights on the block were out. And the dim beams from the others cast eerie shadows on the sidewalk as they made their way to the storefront. Tiny hairs on the back of Heather's neck stood on end.

Chad switched the flashlight on and peeked into the front window of the store. "Can't see anyone," he whispered. He tried the door. "It's locked, but Buddy must be getting in somehow. Let's go around back."

They made their way behind the buildings to a paved parking lot that led all the way to the end of the block of mostly deserted stores. Chad turned the knob on the back door of the empty store. It opened.

He checked the lock. "Broken. This is how he's getting in."

They walked into the back room. The stench of unwashed clothes and rotting food stifled Heather's breath. She puffed out a lungful of the foul-smelling air and rushed to stand by the open door. Chad coughed as he gave the walls and floor a slow scan with his flashlight.

A rickety pallet in the corner of the square room held a thin mattress and a small pillow with an abundance of blankets tossed in a messy pile on top. Old newspapers were stacked a foot high around the bed, like they were somehow protecting it against an unknown predator.

Brown paper and white plastic shopping bags, filled to the brim with used aluminum cans and glass bottles, lined the walls.

Chad set his flashlight on the floor. "Here's an old lantern." He switched it on. "We'll be able to see much better with this."

While it did illuminate more of the filthy room, it only made the place look worse. Heather leaned her head out the back door and inhaled the warm, humid, night air as Chad inspected the area around the bed.

She held her breath, placed a hand over her nose, and ventured back inside.

"Do you see my wallet or a bottle of scotch laying around?" She glanced at the newspapers and picked one up. "Racing forms. My aunt carries one in her purse." *She thinks I don't notice.*

Chad kicked a few blankets off the bed. A man's arm swung out and hit the dirt-encrusted floor.

Chapter 24

HEATHER took a step back. "Is it Buddy?"

Chad pulled off a couple layers of covers, and checked the man's face with the lantern. "Come over here and take a look."

She covered her nose and mouth with her hand as she leaned over. The wild, salt and pepper hair gave him away. "I'm pretty sure it is." One last iota of hope ignited her imagination. "If he's drunk, maybe we can sober him up enough to get some information."

Chad stooped down and felt for a pulse. "We won't get anything out of this guy."

"Why? Has he passed out?"

He looked up at her. "No. He's dead. And from the blood streaming from the wound on his head, I'm pretty sure he was murdered."

Heather's heart hammered in her chest. A shot of adrenaline, sparked by disgust and disappointment, nauseated her. She had to swallow hard to keep her dinner from coming up. The stench in the room added to her discomfort. She ran to the door and sucked in a deep breath of night air. All she wanted to do was get away from there.

Chad came from behind and put a comforting hand on her shoulder as they stepped out into the parking lot.

"I'll call the police." He pulled out his phone and tapped in the number. "This is Chad Willows. There's been a murder at twenty-two Bleaker Street." He kicked a small stone across the parking lot. "I think it's Buddy, the homeless man." After a moment, he made eye contact with Heather. "Yeah, I'll wait here."

Ending the call, he said, "This is gonna put a crimp in Benny's colon. Two murders within a few days of each other."

Is he kidding? Heather stared at him with increasing hostility. "You're concerned about Benny! What about my aunt? This homeless guy was her only hope to find Nikos's killer."

He closed the back door. "I know you're upset. I'm sorry things didn't work out the way you wanted. As a P.I., I've come across plenty of situations like this."

She took a deep breath to cool her rage. He was right. "I'm sorry. I shouldn't take my anger out on you. It's just that I'm worried about my aunt and afraid of who might be killed next."

"Let's hope no one is."

Heather's stomach tightened. She turned away and scanned the parking lot. "We don't know who else is involved. Or who the killer thinks can identify him."

Chad grabbed her shoulders and turned her to face him. "After this murder, the killer will probably lay low for a while. That is, unless they've gotten to the last stage. It's a kind of a swollen egoism where a criminal thinks they're too clever and everybody else is too stupid. And then they start to get careless."

He took his arms down. "Come with me. I've got something that might make you feel better."

As they walked, Heather said, "Nothing will make me feel better, unless you've got Nikos's killer tied up in your back seat with a signed confession in hand."

Chad opened his car door and took two bottles of water and a small white bag from the back seat. He handed her a water bottle.

"Thanks. I could sure use this." She gulped some water to moisten her dry mouth and settle her churning stomach.

He handed her the bag.

She opened it and looked inside. The smell was enough to calm her. A broad smile spread across her lips, even though it seemed inappropriate at a time like this. "Dark chocolate fudge with walnuts?"

"You've had to cope with a lot of problems tonight. You need to eat something sweet before your blood sugar drops. I don't want you passing out on me."

Now that he mentioned it, she had been shaky all evening, but she thought it was just nerves. Taking out a thick square, she bit into the luscious goodness, let it melt in her mouth a moment, and chewed. *Mmm.* "Thanks. This is just what I needed."

Heather handed him the bag back. He pulled out a square and took a bite. As they waited for the police to arrive, she finished hers and pulled a tissue from her pocket to wipe her lips and fingers.

"What do you do, keep a bag of these in your car all the time?"

"Yeah, just for emergencies."

"A likely story."

His lips curved into a half smile. "After Benny asked me to keep an eye on you, I bought some, since I knew these were your favorite."

"That was very thoughtful, and I appreciate it." *Aunt Julia was so wrong about him.* "I need to call my aunt and let her know what happened." She checked the time on her cell. "It's nearly one o'clock. I hope she's not waiting up for me. I should have told her we were coming here."

Chad yawned. "She's probably asleep by now."

"Maybe you're right. I don't need to wake her to give her more bad news. She has to get up early for her first day of community service in a few hours."

A black and white squad car roared up and rocked to a stop. An officer jumped out. A sleek, black sedan followed. Detective Lindsey exited his car and met up with the uniformed officer. The two spoke for a moment before the detective sauntered up to them with his hands on his hips and a frown on his lips.

"So what's this about a murder?"

Chad led him into the back of the store while Heather stayed in the parking lot with the officer. A dull ache throbbed at the base of her skull. She rubbed her neck. *Why do I even bother? It's not going away.* What she needed was to collapse into bed, but she doubted if she'd get much sleep tonight.

Heather recognized the forensics team's van as it pulled into the parking lot. Chad and the detective came out the back door and walked up to meet her as the team entered the building. Detective Lindsey looked from one to the other.

"You wanna tell me what you two are doing here at this time of night, or should I say morning?"

Heather glanced up at Chad, hoping he'd take the hint. She wasn't in any mood to talk with her head pounding.

Chad looked at her, his eyes questioning the pained expression she put on her face. "I was driving Heather back to the hotel from the police station where she reported her wallet stolen—"

"Don't tell me, while you were in the park to meet this guy, where I warned you not to go. Am I right?"

Heather cringed. *Here comes the lecture.* "But my aunt and I had it covered. And Chad was there."

"Now the guy you went to meet, who stole your wallet, has been murdered. What does that tell me?"

"Is that a rhetorical question?" Heather couldn't understand the purpose of it, other than to sound sarcastic. "Because I haven't the faintest idea what it tells you."

The detective tapped his lips in a look of speculation. "Where was your aunt while you were at the police station?"

"She went back to the hotel."

"How do you know where she went?"

"She told me. I talked to her on the phone."

"The hotel phone?"

"No, her cell." Heather didn't like where this conversation was going. "Wait a minute. You can't think she had anything to do with *this* murder."

"Don't tell me what to think, lady."

"I'm not. But if I was, think about this: The person who killed Buddy has to be the same person who killed

Nikos. The way I have it figured is that Buddy was hired to take some drugged wine to my aunt. That means he's the only one who could identify the killer, so he had to be eliminated."

Lindsey shook his head. "I'm not interested in any of your theories, no matter how plausible you make them sound. I've got two very cold bodies and no other suspects than your aunt. So let me do my job."

"Then go in there..." She pointed to the back of the store. "And start detecting."

Lindsey raised an eyebrow. "Listen, most cases are not solved by..." He made quotation marks with his fingers. '*Detecting.*' Somebody makes a slip, or somebody gets a tip. That's usually how it happens. But that doesn't mean I'm not on the job twenty-four seven. Now, go to the station to give the officer your statement. Afterward, I want you to go back to the hotel, and stay there."

Heather grew increasingly irritable with men telling her what to do and what not to do. They all seemed to feel they had the right. Looking from one man to the other, she made an effort for calmness. "Chad, can't you say something to convince him my aunt is innocent?"

His unspoken words hovered uncomfortably in the air for a few moments. Turning around, he ushered her back to his car. She got in the passenger's seat and pulled the door shut with whatever strength she had left. As she leaned her head against the headrest, fatigue tugged at her eyelids. Her head pounded. And her heart ached a little.

Why didn't Chad back up her theories with the detective? She opened the white bag she'd been clutching, broke off a chunk of fudge, and shoved it in her mouth.

Chad put the car in gear and pulled out of the parking lot. Once they were on the street, he glanced at her. "I know what you must think of me, but I didn't want to get into it with Lindsey back there. The tests he took with the gun came back. And I don't need to tell you how they turned out. Now he's got motive, opportunity, and evidence. He was set to arrest your aunt this afternoon. I talked him out of it."

This news perked up her spirits. She swallowed the last of the fudge in her mouth and straightened her back. "You did?"

"For now. But if he finds evidence she has anything to do with this new murder, I won't be able to talk him out of it again."

"Thanks. I appreciate it, and my aunt will too. Personally, I don't think the detective is taking the other suspects seriously. Evidence can be explained by more than one story, you know. Has he tried to make it fit anyone else?"

"He doesn't tell me everything. Maybe we can get Officer Henderson on our side."

Heather doubted that. She sucked in air between her teeth. "I don't think Officer Henderson will be enthusiastic about helping my aunt. She treated him badly when she was in jail overnight."

"Is there anyone your aunt *hasn't* alienated in this town?"

Chapter 25

After they gave their statements to the police, Chad dropped Heather off at the hotel. She waved to Christine at the front desk, took the elevator to the third floor, and trudged to her room. Opening the door, she slipped off her shoes and carried them in.

Heather blinked into the darkness as she tiptoed to her bed, flung the coverlet off, and collapsed onto the mattress in her clothes.

Wrapped in an exhausted sleep, she was transported to a vague, shadowy place where one long nightmarish dream after another, culminated in her aunt being led to the gallows.

"No!" She put a hand to her throat as the sound of her own voice roused her from a deep slumber. Heather's eyelids shot open. The room was bathed in bright sunlight. How could it be morning already? She'd just gone to sleep. She sat up and glanced over to check her aunt's bed. There was no one lying there. Nothing had creased the surface of the flowered coverlet.

Could Aunt Julia have made her bed before she left this morning? She doubted it. Housekeeping took care of that. She turned around to check the time on the bedside clock. Seven-thirty. If Julia got up early to get dressed, why wouldn't she wake her before leaving to do her community service? And why didn't she pull the drapes shut or set the alarm clock before going to bed last night?

What could have happened to Aunt Julia between yesterday evening and this morning? Heather leaped out of bed and hurried to the closet. Her clothes were pushed aside, leaving a gap where her aunt's had been. She checked all the drawers. Julia's things were gone, along with her suitcase. Only one package of tiny mints was left behind on the night stand.

Heather ran to the window, opened it, and looked down at the parking lot below. Her rental car was still there. *I don't understand. Where could Aunt Julia go on foot?*

This didn't make sense. While it was true her aunt lied occasionally like everyone else, she'd always kept her promises. And she promised to stick around this time.

Even though her heart panicked, Heather cautioned herself to maintain a cool, logical mind. She closed the window, picked up the mints, and studied them. Why would Aunt Julia leave these behind? They were almost a part of her. *Unless...* Unless she was forced to pack up and leave. Heather broke out in cold chills right there in the warm May sunshine.

A knock on the door startled her. *Maybe Aunt Julia's back.* She rushed to open it. A tall police officer in uniform stood in the doorway. There was a quiet assurance about Officer Sam Henderson that put her at ease.

"I've come to pick up Julia Fairchild for community service."

Heather put a hand to her forehead. "I almost forgot you were coming this morning. I'm sorry to say, she's gone. And all of her things are, too."

The thin lines around the officer's brown eyes crinkled in suspicion as he glared at her. "Where did she go?"

Heather returned his stare. "I wish I knew."

"So she took off, huh? I'll have to report this." The officer put a hand to his shoulder radio.

"Wait! I don't think she left voluntarily."

He took his hand down. "What makes you say that?"

Heather showed him the package of tiny mints.

"Oh, those."

"Yeah. My aunt is addicted to them. She's always munching on tiny mints. You remember how insistent she was about having them when she spent the night in jail. She'd never leave an entire package behind. And yesterday she promised me she wouldn't run. So that leads me to believe she was forced to go."

The officer crossed his arms. "When was the last time you saw her?"

"Last night around ten-thirty or so. We were in the park—"

"What were you and your aunt doing in the park at ten-thirty at night?"

"It's a long story. Detective Lindsey knows all about it. Anyway, my aunt said she was going right back to the hotel."

"Alone?"

"Yes. She was driving my rental car, and I saw it in the hotel lot this morning."

"And where were *you* going?"

"I stayed behind with Chad Willows."

He raised an eyebrow as his lips curved into a one-sided grin. "I see."

She didn't shrink under his leer. "No you don't. My wallet was stolen. We drove to the station to report it."

Officer Henderson glanced at the flower arrangements lining the walls in the hall, some beginning to wilt. "What's going on here?"

"Derek Kane wanted to impress me."

The officer shook his head. "It figures. Derek's dad owns a huge greenhouse at the edge of town." Still shaking his head, Henderson walked down the hall toward the elevators, stopping a moment to speak into his radio.

Heather couldn't hear what he said. She was too busy trying to find her shoes. Dropping to the floor, she knelt near the bed. Her hand touched a metal object and she pulled it out. "My aunt's binoculars." She grabbed her shoes, her phone, and her nearly empty purse, and ran out the door.

As she slipped into her flats, she waved the binoculars at the officer. "Look what I found."

He glanced at them. "Are these important?"

The elevator doors opened, and they stepped inside. "I don't really know. But my aunt wouldn't leave them behind either."

In the lobby, Heather rushed up to Christine. "I'm glad you're still here."

Christine yawned and blinked tired-looking eyes. "I'm just on my way home. George is due back this morning. We're going out for breakfast and then right to bed."

"I know you're tired..." Heather rubbed the sleep from her own eyes. *So am I.* "Before you go, I'd like to ask you a couple of questions. Did you see my aunt come in last night around ten-thirty?"

"Yes, we talked for a while. She told me what happened in the park." Christine patted Heather's shoulder. "I'm so sorry. I hope the police find your wallet."

"Thanks. I appreciate your concern. Did you see Aunt Julia leave again last night or early this morning?"

"No, but I took a few coffee breaks last night, and I may have dozed off a couple of times. Of course, she could have gone out the side door, and I wouldn't have been able to see her."

"I thought you kept it locked."

"It only locks from the outside, so no one can come in. Anyone can leave that way though. Why?"

"It appears that my aunt left the hotel last night. We're not sure if she did it voluntarily or not."

"I didn't see her leave. I thought she was still in her room this morning."

The officer put his cap on. "Thanks for the information."

Christine came around the front desk and grabbed a copy of the morning newspaper from the counter. She glanced over the front page. "Looks like Frank Kane is going to run against Mayor Bandik in November." She gazed at the ceiling. "If Frank wins, God help this town." She shoved the newspaper under her arm and walked out the door.

Heather let out a breath of frustration. "Derek told me about his dad running against the current mayor. Would it be so bad if he won?"

Sam shrugged. "Frank Kane's been lobbying to tear down those empty storefronts on Bleaker Street to put up a casino. Most of the residents are against it. He's got nearly all the store owners secured. Chad's father is the only one holding out because his daughter, Ashley, wants to build an animal rescue there."

"Do you think the murder of the homeless guy on Mr. Willows's property and my aunt's disappearance could somehow be linked?"

"That's for Detective Lindsey to figure out. I'll just report her as missing for community service. Did she take your car?"

"No, I told you it's still in the parking lot. But all her luggage is missing. She couldn't have made it far on foot. That's why I think someone either forced her to go or somehow convinced her to leave."

"Any idea who that might be?"

"Not at the moment. Who would want to make it look like my aunt was skipping town?"

The officer adjusted his cap with an official flair. "Exactly. But we don't know if anyone has. I'll drive around. Maybe I'll spot her somewhere."

"Thanks. But she could be miles from here by now. You might check with the police in the surrounding towns." Heather put a hand over her mouth as another thought crossed her mind. "Did a train stop here last night?"

"Don't know. You'll have to check."

As Officer Henderson walked out the door, Heather shoved the binoculars in her purse and headed for the breakfast room. She needed a jolt of caffeine to keep her eyes open.

The hotel guests must have already eaten breakfast, the room was empty. She picked up a coffee cup and filled it before going to the buffet where she selected one waffle and two pieces of crisp-looking bacon. Taking her plate to a small table, she sat and took out her cell phone.

As she ate, she scrolled through her emails. Nothing from her aunt. She didn't expect there would be. It was probably useless to call Julia's number. She tried it anyway. It rang and went to voicemail. That figured.

"Hi, Aunt Julia. It's Heather. I'm not angry about you leaving. I'm sure you had your reasons. But please call and let me know where you are and how you are. I'm worried about you. Thanks."

Heather ended the call and checked the train schedule. There were no scheduled stops here last night. And the next train wasn't due until this afternoon.

After breakfast, she darted back to her room, took a quick shower, and changed. Her mind wouldn't stop running through one scenario after another. Where *would* her aunt go? Where *could* she go with no transportation out of town and no driver's license to rent a car?

Maybe someone picked her up. She recalled the telephone call her aunt got the other day. Was it her bookie calling or some old friend Heather had never met? It might have been the guy who gave her the tip on the winning horse. But why would she go willingly when she promised to stick around? Maybe she panicked.

As Heather brushed her hair, her thoughts got crazier. The ringing of her cell shocked her back to the moment. Hands trembling, she answered the call with bated breath.

"Hello?"

"Hi, it's Chad. I'm downstairs. Are you ready to go?"

With her mind on her aunt, she couldn't think why he was there. "Ready to go where?"

"City Hall. Your birth certificate. The DMV?"

She'd completely forgotten about that. "Oh, right. I'll be down in a few minutes."

Since she'd have to have a photo taken for her driver's license, Heather put on a little eye makeup and smoothed her unruly locks, hitting them with a few spritzes of hair spray. She left to catch the elevator. Maybe Chad had some news about her aunt.

The elevator doors opened, and Heather stepped into the hotel lobby. Chad stood at the front desk, having a lively conversation with Vikki, the pretty young clerk. *I suppose he went to school with her, too.*

As Heather walked up to him, he ended the conversation with a tilt of his head and made his way to the door. She walked out of the hotel rubbing her thumbnail along her bottom lip. It always had a soothing effect on her nerves. By the time they reached his car in the parking lot, she'd rubbed off all her gloss.

Chad kept glancing her way. He finally asked, "Are you nervous about something?"

"You might say that." How perceptive of him. "Have you talked to the police this morning?"

"If they found your wallet, they would have called you."

"It isn't my wallet I'm worried about. It's my aunt."

Chapter 26

"WHAT's she done now?"

Heather went over everything in her mind as Chad unlocked his car. "That's just it. She hasn't done anything. My aunt wasn't in our room this morning when Officer Henderson came to pick her up for community service. All her belongings were gone. The only things she left behind were a sealed package of tiny mints and these binoculars." Heather pulled them out of her purse and showed them to Chad. "I can't stop worrying about her."

"Do you have any idea where she might have gone?"

"No. She doesn't have a car, and there was no train out of town last night, so where could she go on foot? And yes... before you suggest it, there's a possibility someone could've picked her up. I've already been through every scenario I can think of with Officer Henderson."

Chad opened the car door for her. "Maybe you and I need to come up with some new scenarios."

She slipped into the passenger's seat. He closed her door and dashed around to the driver's side.

On the way to City Hall, she told him her suspicions about her aunt being coerced into packing up and leaving. He pulled into a parking space in the municipal lot.

"What reason would someone have to do that?"

"All I can think of is that she might have seen the murderer do something that triggered a memory about the night Nikos was killed, and possibly confronted him or her. If that were the case, I'm sure she would've told me."

"Maybe she didn't have time."

Heather opened the car door. "Or someone stopped her from doing it."

***

After Heather secured a certified copy of her birth certificate and a duplicate driver's license, which Chad had loaned her the money for, he dropped her off at the hotel.

"I'd love to stay and talk things over with you, but I'm running late. I have to pick up my sister and open the bookstore. Why don't you come over later? We can brainstorm some ideas about what's happened to your aunt."

"Thanks. I will, around one. And I'll pay you back the money I owe." Heather swung the car door shut and waved at Chad as he drove away.

She ran up to her room, opened her computer, and found her bank's website, but there was no way of getting her money out. Since she'd reported her card stolen last night, her account was frozen. They'd issue her a new card, but it would take five to seven business days, the same as her credit card. She asked them to send the card to her sister's address, since she had no permanent address at the moment.

But she needed money to live on right now. Heather paced the floor. *There must be some way to get cash.*

There was only one person to call. Her sister. The call went to voicemail. At the beep, she explained that her wallet had been stolen and she needed Emily to wire her some cash.

She ended the call and checked her email, deleting the ones from Jack and his loyal minions. She'd sent her resume to so many job sites on Saturday, surely there would be some jobs available in her field by now.

Several opportunities did come up on the screen, but she was either under or over qualified for them. *Why do they even bother sending me those?*

Heather tapped her nails lightly on the computer keys, her patience nearly gone. *I need to put everything into perspective.* The perfect job would eventually turn up. And so would her aunt. The power of positive thinking always worked for her. Well, it made her feel better, anyway.

Her cell rang. She picked it up to hear her sister say, "Sorry to hear about your wallet. Are you okay?"

"Yes. I'm fine. My ATM card and my credit cards are gone, along with all my cash. I reported it to the police, and I've gotten a replacement for my driver's license this morning. The cards will be replaced too, in five to seven days. I had them sent to your address. I hope you don't mind."

"Not at all. I'll wire you money for a train ticket so you can stay with us and wait for them to arrive."

Heather sucked in a gulp of air. "I can't come right now."

"Why not? John and I would love to have you spend some time with us."

"The thing is… Aunt Julia's disappeared."

Emily laughed. "How typical. I thought she might. The woman never could face anything unpleasant. Running away is her forte."

Heather hadn't expected her sister not to take this situation seriously. "But you don't under—"

"I understand she left you holding the bag for her half of the hotel bill. So now you have no reason to be loyal to her any longer."

"But she promised me she'd stick around and face everything this time. And I believed her. I think… I think she may have been forced to pack up and leave. I have to stay here at least for a few more days and try to find her. There's been another murder. She may be in danger."

"Are you serious?" Emily's voice went sober. "I'll wire you some money. I'm not sure how long that will take though. I can't get to it right now. I've got a class to teach in five minutes and another immediately afterward. How much do you think you'll need?"

"At least seven hundred, if you can spare it."

Emily gasped. "I..."

"I know it sounds like a lot, but I've got a few expenses. I'll have to pay the hotel and my rental car before I leave town. Don't worry. I'll pay you back when I get my new cards."

"I know you're good for the money. But for heaven's sake, be careful. Remember who you're dealing with.

Aunt Julia can get herself into some crazy situations. I wouldn't want anything to happen to you, or to her. Call me with progress reports."

"I will, and thanks." Heather ended the call and shot to her feet. Time to get some immediate cash.

She opened her luggage and unzipped her jewelry case. Checking over what little she brought with her, she pulled out the fourteen-karat gold necklace her dad had given her on her sixteenth birthday. A diamond tennis bracelet—the first thing she'd bought for herself when she'd landed her new job, and her grandmother's heirloom sapphire cat pin.

She hated to part with any of them, but she could always buy them back when Emily's transfer came through. Too bad she'd left the exquisite diamond and ruby necklace and matching bracelet Jack had given her, back at the condo they shared. She wouldn't have any qualms about selling those, and she could live like a queen with the money. But knowing how Jack was, he'd probably given them to someone else by now. He was good at recycling.

She wrapped her jewelry in a tissue and opened her purse. The binoculars took up most of the room, so she pushed them aside and placed the items she intended to sell in a side pocket. What was it her aunt said about those binoculars, that they were digital? Could Julia have taken pictures last night?

Heather opened her computer and Googled how to download photos from digital binoculars. She found out she needed a cable to attach them to her USB port. But she didn't want to buy one. They could be expensive. What she needed was a computer geek who already had a cable she could borrow. Too bad she didn't know any here.

On second thought, maybe she did—Chad's sister's friend. What was his name, Kyle something? Oh well, it didn't matter. She'd already asked so much of the Willows family. How could she ask them for one more favor?

She rubbed her thumbnail across her bottom lip, trying to decide. In this case, yes, she'd do it. Anything to help find her aunt. Maybe she'd see something significant in the photos. That is, if Julia had taken any.

Heather closed her laptop and threw her purse straps over her shoulder. Sprinting to her car, she drove to the only jeweler in town, where she sold her precious items to a reluctant store manager who offered her half of what they were worth. She needed cash now, so she accepted the small amount of money, and left.

The time on her car radio read, 1:10. She'd stop at the bookstore. Maybe this computer geek guy was there. Her stomach rumbled from hunger. She should grab lunch first, but she didn't want to spend the money. She had to pay Chad what she owed him, so she'd skip lunch this afternoon and have a big dinner instead. Hopefully her sister would have sent the money to Western Union by then.

Heather pulled her car up to the front of the bookstore and got out. As she opened the front door, the bell tinkled, and once again, Makkie greeted her with a loud *meow*. He rubbed his face against her hand as she raised it to pet him, and her heart melted. She was getting very fond of that sweet, green-eyed cat—and this quaint old bookstore. Not to mention, the owners.

There was no mistaking the squeak of Ashley's wheelchair as it rounded the corner. "Hi Heather. Chad said you'd be stopping by. We were just having lunch. Why don't you join us? He ordered Chinese, and there's so much, I don't think we can finish it all. You haven't eaten have you?"

"No, I haven't. Thanks, I'd love to join you." Heather followed Ashley into the back room.

Chad stood behind the container-covered desk. He turned away when he saw her and rubbed the back of his neck.

Something's wrong. "What is it?"

He turned back to look at her. "Lindsey just told me Buddy was killed between seven and nine last night. So he couldn't have met you in the park at ten."

A cold chill ran down Heather's spine. Her knees weakened, and she dropped into a chair across from the desk. "Oh, my God! I thought he was killed later, like after he got home from the park."

Ashley wheeled up to her and put a comforting arm around her shoulders. "Are you okay?"

"Yes, thanks." Heather channeled her aunt and put on a brave face. She glanced up at Chad. "If it wasn't Buddy, then who?"

"That's what Detective Lindsey was asking me on the phone when you walked into the store. I told him you'd be here, so he's on his way over to question you."

Heather opened her purse and took out the binoculars. "There may be a clue as to who it was on this." She handed them to Chad.

He held the binoculars up to his eyes. "Digital?"

"Yes, and I think my aunt may have taken pictures of whoever stole my purse."

Chad set the binoculars on the table and closed one of the half-empty white cartons. "I'll clear this desk. We can eat later."

The smell of Chinese food wasn't doing Heather's upset stomach any good. *Stop thinking about food.* "Before Detective Lindsey gets here, can we check to see if my aunt took any photos with those binoculars?"

Chad put the last of the containers in the refrigerator, and came over to sit in the computer chair. "Where's the cable for these?"

"I don't have one. Do you have a cable that might fit?"

"I don't know if you can use just any cable. You might need the one that came with the binoculars."

Heather huffed. "Well, so much for that."

Ashley grabbed the binoculars. "Wait. I've got an idea." She tapped on her cell phone, and put it to her ear as she rolled into the bookstore.

Heather's stomach grumbled. She couldn't help glancing at the refrigerator. *Maybe if I just ate one eggroll.* It grumbled again, louder. She checked her cell phone, pretending not to notice.

The sounds must have caught Chad's attention, because he came up to her. "I'm sorry. Where are my manners? Would you like something to drink?"

"I'd love a soft drink." At least the carbonation would calm her stomach for a while.

He opened the fridge and handed her a can of Pepsi. "Is this all right?"

"Yes. Thank you." She popped the top and took a couple of sips. As soon as the first swallow hit her stomach, it settled down a bit.

Ashley wheeled back into the room. "I just talked to Kyle. He said we have a cable that might fit these binoculars." She opened the bottom desk drawer and pulled out a clear plastic bag with assorted cables. "Try one of these."

Chad pulled out a thin white cable and connected one side to the binoculars. "This one might do." He connected the other end to the USB drive on his desk-top. Heather couldn't breathe as she waited for the photos to download onto the screen.

But no photos came up.

"This is disappointing." Her hopes sank. "Now what?"

Ashley wheeled her chair closer to the desk. "Don't give up yet. Kyle checked out this model of digital binocular on his laptop. He said it has an instant replay video feature that allows the user to save the last five to sixty seconds of whatever they were watching."

Chad used his mouse to click on the screen. "Here's the video."

It showed Heather standing in the park near the bridge. The next moment, a tall man wearing a gray raincoat with the collar pulled up approached Heather and whacked her left side with the paper shopping bag he carried. She stumbled. End of video.

"This must have been when Aunt Julia dropped the binoculars and drove my rental car over the grass to get to me. Could you play it again?" Heather asked. "We might be able to recognize the man."

"Okay," Chad said. "But it's too dark to see his face. Maybe the police can decipher who he is. They have much better equipment."

No sooner had he said the words than the doorbell jingled and Detective Lindsey strolled into the room.

Chapter 27

HEATHER ran up to the detective. "Chad just told me Buddy was killed between seven and nine last night. At that time, my aunt and I were having dinner at the hotel. You can ask the desk clerk, Vikki. She spoke with us. And afterward we delivered some flowers to the retirement village. You can ask the manager there, too. So it proves my aunt couldn't possibly have killed Buddy."

Detective Lindsey rubbed his forehead. "Slow down. I'll check it out. But if that's true, why did she pack up and skip town this morning?"

"Like I told Officer Henderson, I think she was forced to go, to make it look like she was guilty of murder and she was running away. Take a look at this."

Chad reran the video, and the detective watched as Heather explained, "My aunt took this with her digital binoculars. Plus, she chased the man for about a half-block before he dropped my purse, so I think she may have seen his face or else she saw someone who shouldn't have been there."

Chad unplugged the cable and handed the binoculars to Detective Lindsey.

"Okay, you've convinced me. I'll give you the benefit of the doubt. We'll go on the assumption she was forced to leave the hotel. She may still be in town. I'll have every available man looking for her. If she's here, we'll find her."

***

After the detective left, Chad heated their Chinese takeout in the microwave and set it on the desk. Heather munched on an eggroll but could barely swallow the last bite. Her stomach was as unsettled as her mind. She stood and paced the room as she sipped the last of her Pepsi. Chad and Ashley picked at their food and finally put their forks down.

Heather needed to do something to keep herself busy while she waited for word from Detective Lindsey. "Are you finished?" she asked them.

"I think we are," Chad said.

She grabbed the white lunch cartons and paper plates and tossed them in the trash. A heaviness settled on her heart. She couldn't explain this feeling. It was a massive foreboding—like waiting for a disaster, you weren't prepared for, to strike.

There was no way she could hang around the bookstore all afternoon and do nothing while God only knew what was happening to her aunt. She needed air, but she also needed a change of plans.

Heather grabbed her purse. "I'm going to drive around town. Aunt Julia left me her mints and the binoculars. Maybe she left more clues. I just need to find them."

Chad leaped out of his chair. "Wait! I'll go with you."

As they scurried out of the room, he said, "I think it's best if we split up. I'll take the retirement village and Bleaker Street. You take the park and the hotel area. We can meet back here at..." He checked the time on his cell. "Let's say between four-thirty and five if we don't find anything. If we do, we can call each other and—"

"Stop!" Ashley's shrill voice cut off his next word. "Just look at you. You're two of a kind. Ready to run all over town, chasing any misguided clue you might encounter, instead of thinking things out rationally." She caught a breath. "You'd waste a lot less time if you narrowed everything down to a few obvious places Julia might be."

Chad spun around to look at his sister. "Since when did you become the voice of reason?"

"Since you let your feelings about... " Ashley glanced at Heather. "... *this situation* make you less objective."

A blush worked its way up from his neck and tinged his cheeks. "Just because you're my sister, that doesn't give you the right..."

An embarrassed heat warmed Heather's cheeks. *Change of subject time.* She came back to the desk, set her purse on top, and eased herself into a chair. "I suppose Ashley's right about narrowing places down instead of running all over town."

Chad circled the desk and sat opposite her. Ashley rolled up next to him. "Okay," she said. "Where do we start?"

"There's no *we*." Chad gave his sister a sideways glance. "*You* go back into the store and take care of the customers. Heather and I will work on this."

Ashley rolled her wheelchair toward the door. "Not fair. It was my idea."

"You and I will have this out later," he said. "Right now, there are more important things to talk about." He turned to Heather, his eyes softening. "Tell me where you suspect your aunt might be. I'm pretty sure we can rule out Chicago, unless she had some way of getting there."

Heather dragged her hands over her face. "And if she contacted my sister, Emily would have called me. I firmly believe she wouldn't leave on her own, so she must have left with someone she knew from here. But she doesn't know that many people in town, except for the people at your party, and the people who work at the hotel."

Of course. Why hadn't she thought of it sooner? "The hotel!"

"What about the hotel?"

"Not the hotel itself, but the guests who stayed there on Friday night. This may all be hypothetical, but the man who my aunt dated, your former boss Henry Rankin, had two children in their early thirties. She didn't think they knew about her affair with their father. But what if they did, and they thought she was responsible for his death?"

Chad leaned back in his chair. "This puts a whole new light on the subject."

Heather couldn't stop herself as the words poured out. "What if they tracked her down and were on the train with us? They would have been at the hotel that night. Maybe even in the bar when my aunt had the heated argument with Nikos."

"We need more than just speculation to go on. Besides, nearly everyone who stayed at the hotel that night was cleared by the police and took the next train out of town. So she couldn't have gone off with any of them."

"Cleared by the police, huh?" Another idea struck her. "The police! How well you do know your ex-uncle?"

"Benny? He's okay. But I have to admit, I don't know much about him these days. At least, not since my aunt divorced him and moved to Chicago."

"Is there a way you can check into his finances? Maybe he's in desperate need of money. I mean, he might have killed Nikos for the winning ticket. Being a detective, he must handle guns all the time. And he's in a perfect position to frame my aunt. Right now he could be holding her somewhere so it appears she's run away. Who else would she trust enough to go off with?"

Chad shook his head. "But how would he know Buddy?"

"He was in jail the same time as my aunt. Detective Lindsey could have cut him a deal, and of course, then he would have had to kill him." She stood and paced the floor.

"No!" Chad shot to his feet. "That's ridiculous. I can't believe it."

She grabbed her purse. "Believe or don't believe whatever you want. I've got to go and look for my aunt."

"Wait." Chad's hand grasped her shoulder. "This is complete conjecture. You have no evidence that proves Benny's the killer."

She jutted out her chin and met his eyes. "Then I need to get some. You know the people in this town better than I do. How do you suggest I go about getting evidence? That is, if you're still willing to help me."

"I am." He took his hand down. "I've got friends on the force. I'll ask if they know anything about his finances. But that's as far as it can go. I still think you're making a mistake."

"At the very least, we can eliminate him as a suspect. Think of where he could possibly have taken my aunt. Is there a basement in his house or an old shed on his property?"

"He sold the house he and my aunt were living in as part of the divorce settlement. I'm not sure where he's living now. But I'll find out. And I'll check the area near the jail, too. There's an old, abandoned warehouse around the corner."

"You do that. Meanwhile, I'll snoop around inside the hotel. My aunt might be in one of the empty rooms. Could she be in a place so obvious that everyone's overlooked it?"

Chad grinned. "You know what Sherlock Holmes said, 'There's nothing more deceptive than an obvious fact.'"

A mystery fan. Looks like we have something in common besides fudge.

Chad picked up his cell phone and walked her toward the front door. "Keep in touch. I don't want you disappearing, too."

"Don't worry. I can take care of myself." Heather said the words, but more self-doubt chipped away at her confidence every day.

Chapter 28

CONFLICTING thoughts about whether her aunt was forced to leave or if she left on her own had Heather taking the long way back to the hotel. As a yellow traffic signal turned red, she hit the brakes, and a small newspaper slid out from under the passenger seat. Heather picked up the racing form.

Her suspicions were confirmed. Aunt Julia *had* been playing the horses. Why would her aunt leave this paper in the car for her to find when she'd been so secretive about it up until now? Could this be another clue?

Heather drove past the off-track betting parlor but couldn't resist the urge to pull into an empty parking space around the corner. She got out of the car and walked through the alley behind the building, and just as before, she peeked in the back window. Nothing moved inside. She turned the doorknob. Locked. A strange sense of desperation seized her, and she pounded on the door. "Aunt Julia, are you in there?"

She peered through the window again on the off-chance she might see her aunt or at least Krystal Stamos. Everything was still. And then a shadow moved across the glass. She jumped back, startled.

Tapping on the window, she shouted, "Hello?"

At least she'd be able to ask whomever was inside if they'd seen her aunt. The door swung open, and she was face to shoulder with Derek Kane. She looked up into his disarming smile.

"What are you doing here?" he asked.

Heather's heart raced. She hadn't expected *him* to be in there. "I... um. I'm looking for my aunt. She seems to have disappeared either last night or early this morning. Have you seen her?"

Derek put out a welcoming hand. "Come in."

Thank goodness it was him and not Krystal. She wasn't in any mood to spar with her this afternoon. At least Derek might be able to help. She walked in and gave a cautious glance around. "Is Krystal here?"

He closed the door, and the locked clicked in place. "No. She has some relatives coming in from out of town. She's meeting them for a family dinner and some kind of private service for her dad. Not sure what that is, so she won't be around until after the funeral."

"I see. So what are you doing here at um...? She checked the time on her cell. "Five o'clock? Shouldn't you be working at the hotel?"

"No, my hours are six to midnight now that this place is closed. But Krystal asked me to do a bar inventory before she opens for the Derby on Saturday." He escorted Heather into the next room and seated her at the bar. "Since this would be happy hour if we were open, why not have a couple of drinks on me?"

"No thanks. I'll just have bottled water." She needed to stay sober.

"Still with the water? Suit yourself, but you're missing some pretty awesome concoctions."

As he grabbed water from the refrigerator and poured it in a clear glass, Heather scanned the dozens of colored liquor bottles lined up against the back wall. She couldn't help noticing there were two bottles of scotch. An open one in front of another.

She kept glancing at it trying to see the label behind the first bottle. Too bad she didn't have a clear view. "I've changed my mind. Add a shot of scotch to that water. Single malt, if you have it." She crossed her fingers. *Please don't let it be my bottle back there.*

"Sorry, there's no ice," he said. "Is neat okay?"

"Fine."

Derek stretched his arm behind him to grab the scotch. He checked the label. "This isn't the single malt." He put it back and picked up the other bottle. After opening it, Derek shoved a pour spout into the top. Then he poured a shot into her water and placed the glass in front of Heather. "I would never have taken you for a scotch drinker."

She couldn't take her eyes off the label as he set the bottle back on the shelf. It had the exact same rip in it as the one she'd bought for Buddy. Her heart sank. What were the odds of two bottles with the exact same part of the label missing? She couldn't control the tremble in her hand as she took a sip of her drink.

Ugh! She hated scotch.

Who else would have access to this bar? Krystal, for one. But would she be involved in her own dad's murder? This was something she hadn't really considered. She'd have to discuss it with Chad and Detective

Lindsey. But since Derek was handy, he might know something.

"You never answered my original question. Did you see my aunt last night or this morning?"

He looked her straight in the eye. "No, I can't say I have. Julia's quite a character, isn't she? I mean, disappearing like that?"

As if he hadn't encouraged the woman to run off. Come to think of it, he didn't seem surprised when she told him. She logged that little tidbit away and continued her line of questioning.

"Were the Stamoses a happy family?"

"Where did that question come from? Aren't you worried about your aunt?"

"I am. But I was just wondering."

"As far as I know, they argued quite a bit. At least, that's what Krystal told me when we were in high school. Her dad was kind of strict. So, she'd sneak out a lot."

Heather took another sip of her drink. *Ugh!* "And what about her mom? Was she strict too?"

"Her mom seemed nice. She passed away when Krystal was sixteen. After that, she and her dad fought all the time, until she and Chad got engaged, then things seemed to quiet down between them. Most likely, Chad's influence. But the engagement... big mistake. I saw that breakup coming a mile away. Chad hates being tied down, unlike me." He winked. "If the right woman came along, I wouldn't hesitate to marry her."

She hoped he didn't consider *her* the right woman. *I'm not ready for another relationship like the one I just ended.* "Do you think Krystal hated her dad enough to kill him or have him killed?"

He snickered. "I wouldn't be surprised."

Heather's cell vibrated in her pocket. She peeked at it. Jack. Ignoring the call, she went back to questioning Derek. "So you think she might be involved?"

"There's a definite possibility."

Her cell vibrated again. She gave it a quick glimpse. This time it was Chad. Without letting Derek know she needed to tell Chad this new information, she slipped off her stool and gave him a casual, warm smile. "Will you excuse me? I'll be right back."

Derek lifted his chin. His eyes sparkled in the overhead light from the bar. "I'll be waiting."

She headed toward the ladies' room. As she passed through the hall, her shoe crunched a small object on the floor. She lifted her foot. "What is that, a piece of chalk?" She bent over and scraped it off her heel with a tissue. But the smell was unmistakable—peppermint! Heather did a quick search of the floor and found two more leading to a side door.

Her heart raced as she checked her missed calls and tapped Chad's name in her missed call log. It rang a few times and went to voicemail.

"I'm glad you called me. I've got information. That bottle of scotch I bought for Buddy is here. And I found some of my aunt's mints on the floor in the hall. I'm at—"

A strong hand clamped over her mouth as cold metal was shoved into her back. "Drop the phone."

She put her arm down and let the cell slip to the floor. Derek took his hand from her mouth and grabbed her arm. Heather twisted it from his restraining grasp. She looked behind him at the bar area, her best shot at freedom. Her pepper spray was in her purse, but she'd wait for a better opportunity, like when he was a few feet away and couldn't take it from her.

Derek's lips curled into a sneer. "From the look on your face when you saw that bottle of scotch, I thought you might have recognized it."

"You mean the bottle you stole from me at the park, Derek? Right after you murdered Buddy? Did you kill Nikos too?" She spoke as loudly as she could without being too obvious. Maybe Chad's voicemail was still recording.

Derek raised his knee and smashed her phone with one stomp, crushing her hopes along with it. "I had no choice. I told you I worked in the mayor's office. I've been borrowing city funds to bankroll my gambling. I owed Nikos thousands I couldn't pay back, and he threatened to go to the media if I didn't come up with the money. That would have ruined not only my career, but my dad's chances of getting elected mayor."

He poked her back, giving Heather a shove. "Walk *that* way." She stumbled forward a few steps.

Derek opened the door to a small office. "I'd been putting Nikos off for weeks. Friday evening, your aunt came in here and dropped her derringer on the bar. I couldn't pass up an opportunity like that. Talk about being in the right place at the right time."

Heather walked in and scanned the room. Her aunt was bound and gagged in a wooden chair next to the large mahogany desk, her wrists secured to the arms with plastic zip ties. Heather rushed over to her.

Julia's eyes flashed a look of hope.

"I've been so worried. Are you okay?"

Julia scrunched her eyes and stared at Derek as he moved behind the desk and turned on the computer. He came around the front and shoved Heather toward the desk, pushing her down into the chair.

Tilting her head back, Heather's eyes met his with a calm, steady gaze. "What are going to do with us?"

"I'm giving you a chance to win enough money for me to put it all back, before anyone finds out it's missing. I saw your aunt pick a winning horse before. Nikos had her ticket, but it wasn't on him, and I don't know what he did with it. Now I want another winning horse."

Heather pulled herself up in the chair and set a fist on each hip. "Why should she pick a winning horse for you?"

"Because if she doesn't, I'll kill *you*." Derek turned the computer screen so both she and her aunt could see the names of the horses and the odds. "Get started."

"Why don't you take the tape off so my aunt can give you a name, herself?"

"Oh no." Derek shook his head. "Her yammering drove me crazy! That's why I put tape on in the first place." He checked the time on his phone and held the gun to Heather's head. "The minutes are ticking away. You'd better figure it out, *now!*"

Heather stared at all the information and tried to determine which horse had the best chance of winning.

What did Chad tell her? *The odds, always the odds.* Too bad she didn't know what he meant by that.

"Choose carefully. The race starts in five minutes." Derek grabbed his cell and tapped in a number. "My bookie."

Heather ran a hand through her hair. "This is crazy! What if she can't do it?"

He set his phone down and gazed into her eyes as his lips curved into a sly grin. "She'd better, because this isn't just an ordinary race. *You'll* be betting your lives on it."

Taking a deep, unsteady breath, Heather swallowed hard. She lifted her chin, meeting his icy gaze straight on. "You don't intimidate me." *Much.*

She moved her gaze to her aunt. "Which one?"

Julia blinked wildly and nodded toward the desk, obviously trying to give her a clue.

"Four minutes." Derek paced the floor as he spat out the words with a taunting glee to his voice. "Better hurry."

Heather scanned the names of the horses and tried to associate them with what was on the desk: *computer screen, pen, papers, clips, calendar.* Her fingers ran feverishly over the old wood. There were no horse names associated with anything there. What was her aunt trying to tell her?

She looked at her aunt again. "I need a better clue."

Julia held up three fingers.

Heather scrolled through the horses' names again. *Of course!* Her mind finally made the connection. *I hope Aunt Julia knows what she's doing.*

"Two minutes before the race starts." Derek's voice was stern. "You're out of time!"

Heather sucked in a deep breath, crossed her fingers, and blurted out, "The number three horse. Brown-eyed Girl."

Derek scoffed, "The big bucks are split between the favorites, and that nag is a thirty-to-one long shot. She hasn't come near the money in her last six tries. Are you sure?"

Julia gave a terse nod.

"Yes." Heather said it with a confidence she didn't really feel. But her aunt's eyes blinked their approval, and that was good enough for her.

Derek put his cell phone to his ear. "Six big ones on the number three horse's nose." He ended the call and switched the computer screen over to the race.

A moment later, the buzzer sounded, and the horses were out of the gate in a blur of frantic movement. Heather's stomach tightened as she screamed, "Come on Brown-eyed Girl," with every turn around the dirt track. Finally, she held her breath as two horses raced neck-and neck toward the finish line.

The whole event lasted less than two minutes, yet with her life on the line, it felt like an eternity.

Chapter 29

THE race ended in a photo finish between Brown-eyed Girl and the number two horse, Max's Dream. The announcer said, "The winner of the third race is ... Max's Dream."

Derek kicked the desk and slammed his hand against it as he swore under his breath.

Julia shook her head like a wild woman. Her brows scrunched down to touch her eyelids.

Heather's hope sank along with her posture. Her brain was cognizant of the fact they'd lost, but she wouldn't let her heart believe it. She'd have to make a run for the door before the shock of losing wore off, and Derek came to his senses. She might just make it if...

The announcer's face came back on the screen. "Hold on to your tickets. Max's Dream has been disqualified for interference. The winner of the third race is Brown Eyed Girl."

Heather squared her shoulders and glanced at her aunt. Julia looked visibly relieved.

Derek turned off the computer and waved the gun in Heather's face. "Well, you picked the winner, after all. Lucky you and lucky me. I can finally pay off my debts. Unfortunately, there's no way I can let you live. Not with everything you know about me."

Maybe she could convince him that killing them would be a bad idea, but she reminded herself he was probably a psychopath. He wouldn't even consider letting them go. And no one would ever suspect him of murder—not with that smile of his. She'd already lost so much, all she had left was her dignity and her life, and she wasn't about to let Derek take those away, too.

Heather rolled the desk chair back and dug around in her purse for the pepper spray. Derek took the small black container out of his pocket and held it up. "Looking for this? I took it out when you were picking a horse. I noticed it in there when I stole your purse."

A streak of red crossed Heather's eyes. Setting her feet firmly on the floor for traction, she gritted her teeth, and with frenzied determination, she shot out of the chair, catching Derek's arm and knocking the gun out of his hand. It thudded on the tile.

They both dropped to their knees in a race to grab it. Julia rattled her chair sideways, moving it a few inches, and kicked the gun out of Derek's reach. It slid across the floor. Heather scrambled to get it. Derek grabbed her leg and pulled her down. He leaped over her to get there first. Snatching up the gun, he pointed it at her.

"Stay down!" His mouth twisted into a wry grin. "You really surprised me, Miss Stanton. I didn't think you had the guts to fight back. It was so easy to knock you off your feet last night. I would've done worse if your aunt hadn't almost run me over."

He pointed a finger at Julia. "I wasn't sure if she recognized my face when I turned to glance at her, so I had to make sure she was out of the picture. After she gave me the winning horse in today's race, I was going to convince you she'd run away and was killed by a hit and run driver as she walked along a lonely stretch of back road. Until you came snooping around here."

Heather's heart pounded. She shuddered and released a soft scoff. "And of course, you had to get rid of Buddy, too."

"Yeah, well, he told me he was going to meet you at the park and spill his guts unless I came up with some pretty substantial hush money. He was just a loose end. Men like him are always expendable."

His voice held an undertone of cold contempt. There would be no reasoning with him. Heather cringed at how much evil Derek might be capable of.

He pulled back the trigger on the gun. Julia rattled her chair and shrieked. Derek's eyes grazed her for a moment. "Shut up old lady, or I'll kill you first."

This gave Heather time to scoot behind the desk. *Bam!* The searing hot trajectory passed inches from her head, striking the chair cushion.

The door flew open and hit Derek in the back, knocking him off balance. He regained his footing and swung around to face Chad.

"Gimme the gun," Chad said.

Derek snorted his disbelief. "The only way you're getting this gun is if you wrestle me for it. And we both know you were never in my league."

With a sharp, quick action, Chad grabbed Derek's wrist with both his hands and twisted the arm holding the gun behind Derek's back. He took the gun. "I wasn't very good at wrestling, so I took up Karate."

Detective Lindsey rushed in behind Chad. "I told you to wait for us." The detective put out his hand. "I'll take that."

Chad handed him the gun as Officer Henderson walked in and slapped handcuffs on Derek, reading him his rights.

There was a visible lessening of tension on Julia's face as she slouched down in the chair. Heather let out a long, slow sigh and, with wobbly knees, made it to her feet. "Thank goodness you got my voice mail."

Chad grasped both her arms, his gaze riveted on her face. "I came as soon as I could, but I didn't know you were in this room until I heard the gun shot. I'm so relieved you're not hurt. For a minute there, I thought I might have lost you."

"I'm okay. Just a little..." As stark reality hit, a bitter cold overcame Heather, and she couldn't stop shaking.

He pulled her into a tight embrace. "You're in shock. It'll wear off soon."

Heather nestled her face deep in his shoulder, tears of relief soaking into his white shirt. She lingered there, resting against the warm lines of his body and welcoming the comfort of his arms.

Detective Lindsey took care removing the duct tape from Julia's mouth and cutting the restraints from her wrists.

She jumped to her feet and raised a fist in the air. "Wait until I get my hands on that maniac, I'm gonna knock him every way to Sunday!"

Lindsey's eyebrows furled as he grabbed her arm before she could take a step. "Calm down, Mrs. Fairchild. You're not doing anything to anyone."

Julia rubbed her raw cheeks. "I'm so angry, I could spit!" She inched closer to Lindsey. "I'd be a lot calmer if you took me out for a drink. I could really use one after what I've been through."

"I'll bet you can, but the only place you're going is to the station house to make a statement." He escorted her to the door. "Lady, you've been a thorn in my side almost since the day you got here."

Julia curved her red, swollen lips into a tight grin and batted her eyelashes at the detective. "You don't mean that."

Heather couldn't believe her aunt's resilience. A few moments ago, she was facing death at the hands of a psychopath, and now she was flirting with the detective.

Chad lifted her chin, bringing her face close to his, like he was going to kiss her. She was sure he would. Every fiber of her being wanted him to. Her pulse quickened with eager anticipation.

His lips parted.

Her eyelids fluttered shut.

"Are you ready to get out of here?" He whispered.

Her eyelids shot open. She dropped her shoulders and breathed a quiet, "Yes."

Chapter 30

HEATHER closed her eyes in bed that night. But after reliving her story over and over at the police station while wolfing down a cheeseburger and fries from The Club Car Diner, frazzled nerves and a knotted stomach wouldn't allow sleep to come.

Her restless mind raced with thoughts of the afternoon's events, mingled with thoughts of Chad, his face haunting her: smiling, serious, thoughtful. She didn't know much about him personally, except he had the bluest eyes she'd ever seen, and he seemed perpetually amused at life. Something about him drew her in when he turned on that boyish charm.

She filtered back to the day she'd met him, so handsome, so virile. He could be strong and yet tender. As she recalled the thrill of being held against his muscular body, her own ached with desire.

As much as she'd love to be a part of his life, if he was commitment-phobic, like Derek said, could she ever have a future with him? While Chad seemed concerned about her welfare last night, he didn't say goodbye when they left the station. She wished she could hang around here and—but this was no time to be thinking about him. No time to admit to herself she might be falling for a man she'd probably never see again.

Silent tears rolled down her cheeks. She sniffled and wiped them away. She was used to being let down. Why should he be any different from the other men in her life?

She had to stop thinking of him, so she switched her thoughts to the immediate future. What were her options—keep running away, or go back to some semblance of her life in Chicago? She didn't want to do either, but she'd have to make a decision soon. After paying the hotel and the car rental, there wouldn't be much left to live on. She rolled over and finally dozed off into an uneasy sleep.

***

Buzz. Heather opened her eyes and switched off the alarm clock. After the restless night she'd had, morning came as a relief.

Julia sat up in bed and rubbed her eyes. "Ugh, is it time to get up already?"

"I'm afraid so." Heather pulled the covers over her head. She wasn't ready to face the day just yet.

"What are *you* afraid of? You should be excited. This is the first day of the rest of your new life!"

What new life? Why was her aunt so upbeat this morning? Heather peeked over the top of the covers. "I thought it was the first day of your community service sentence."

"It is. And I have to look especially nice." Julia made her way to the small closet and looked through her clothes. "Benny... I mean, Detective Lindsey is picking me up for a quick breakfast, and then he's taking me to my first assignment. Is that what they call it—an assignment? Not sure." She rummaged through her shoes and picked out a pair of white sneakers. "Yeah, I can wear these. He said I should be comfortable."

Heather sat up in bed and swung her legs over the side. "When did you get so friendly with Detective Lindsey?"

Julia selected her scarlet-flowered summer blouse and a pair of white pants. She sauntered toward the bathroom. "We spent so much time at the station last night, talking, that one thing led to another, and umm ... You know how it is when you have a lot in common with someone?"

"Yeah, I know." Heather got up and followed her aunt. "There's one thing I didn't get a chance to ask you about last night. How could you be so sure Brown Eyed Girl was going to win that race yesterday afternoon?"

Julia spun around. "Years of experience." She raised her eyebrows. "And a little inside information."

"So you knew that horse was going to win even before the race started?"

"Well..." Julia moved her hand in a see-saw motion. "I wasn't one hundred percent sure. Let's just say I had a pretty good idea."

Heather wagged a finger at her aunt. "One of these days, you have to do something about your gambling addiction."

"My dear niece, what you need to recognize is the difference between an addiction and a predilection, which is what I have."

Heather could only shake her head.

At a loss for what to do today, she sifted through the few clothes she'd brought with her. A white tee and jeans were good enough to hang around the hotel and check her emails for available jobs. She meandered over to the desk and unplugged her phone from the charger. It rang. Checking the caller ID, her heart skipped a beat.

"Chad... Hi."

"How are you feeling this morning?" His tone had a degree of warmth and concern.

"Tired, but otherwise I'm fine. And you?"

"I'm good. Listen, Benny's on his way over to pick up your aunt, so if you don't have any other plans, I thought you might like to go out for breakfast."

Heather smiled to herself. "I'd love to."

"Great," he said. "How long will it take you to get dressed?"

"Just give me ten minutes or so."

"I'm starting for the hotel now. I'll meet you in the lobby."

She ended the call and sat there absently holding the phone in her hand, thinking about Chad, wishing she understood him.

Julia opened the bathroom door. "Was that Benny?"

"No, it was Chad Willows."

Julia smirked as she strutted toward her niece. "You like that young man, don't you?"

Heather couldn't help the grin that lit up her face. "Yes. I like him very much. I'm not sure if the feeling's mutual."

Julia set her fists on her hips. "Have you ever given him any encouragement? From what I've seen, you've been playing it pretty cool, like you always do. Are you worried he'll turn out to be another Jack Steele?"

She *had* acted cool toward Chad, but it was unintentional, at least most of the time. "I don't think he's anything like Jack. And you're right, I've been a little standoffish, partly because I didn't trust him for a while, and the other part is because you told me you thought he looked like a con man."

"It just goes to show, never judge a man by the way someone else thinks he looks. He's proven himself to be a good guy, hasn't he?"

"He has."

"Then, like I've said before, sometimes you have to take a chance." Julia strolled to the desk and opened her purse.

"Chad lives here, and I'm going back to Chicago, so what's the point? Long distance relationships hardly ever work." Heather grabbed her hair brush.

"Then move here. It's not like Chicago has much to offer you these days. Plus, I'll be stuck in this town for quite a while, and I've spent so little time with you." Julia tipped her head to the side. Tears welled in her eyes as her bottom lip quivered. "Please don't leave me here alone."

The pleading look on her aunt's face touched Heather's heart.

"If I moved here, what would I do, work at Dutch's gym or be a server in Mayor Bandik's restaurant?"

Julia sniffed and wiped her nose with a tissue. "Do what you did in Chicago."

"I was an account executive at a marketing firm. In case you haven't noticed, there aren't any jobs like that in this town."

"Why can't you do marketing from your laptop? Everybody's on the internet these days. You're creative. Put your talents to work for yourself instead of for someone else. Besides, you don't want the hassle of going back to a high-pressure job like the one you just quit, do you?"

At this point in her life, Heather didn't think she could handle it. "I can't say I've been looking forward to getting back to the daily grind." She paced the floor in short, quick steps as she rubbed her thumbnail across her bottom lip. "I don't know. It would be a huge change for me." She was used to living the good life. Now she'd have to tighten her belt and scrimp.

"So, take a chance on this too. You don't have that much to lose, and you might just have everything to gain."

"But I need cash to live on. Setting myself up in online marketing would take money, and it'll be a while before I'll see any kind of profit."

"That reminds me." Julia stuck her hand in her purse and took out a check. She handed it to Heather. "Here's what I owe you, plus compounded interest."

Heather's jaw dropped as she read the large dollar amount. "Where did you get all this?"

"The thought of having to live on the street while I served out my sentence terrified me, so I called in a huge favor. It only took a couple of phone calls."

"I offered to help support you."

"I know, but I couldn't ask you to do that. So I placed everything I could beg, borrow, or haggle away from the pawn broker on Brown Eyed Girl in the fifth race yesterday. If you'll recall, that horse paid thirty-to-one. I instructed my bookie not to place my bet until the last minute so the odds wouldn't go down."

"I can't take all this. It's too much."

"Sure you can. You helped me out when I needed it. Just consider it a loan, or an investment in your future, if you like. I trust you to pay me back, just like you trusted me to pay you back."

Heather's heart lightened as she put the check in the room safe. She'd transfer the money to her bank, later. Today really *could* be the first day of the rest of her new life.

Julia's eyes squinted as her lips pressed together in a determined look. "I'm still going to find a way to get my hands on the money Nikos stole from me. My winning ticket has to be somewhere in this town. Or else he converted it to cash and stashed it. You mark my words: I'm going to find either one or the other."

Knowing her aunt's tenacity, Heather didn't doubt that for a second. She threw her arms around Julia's neck and gave her a hug. "You're incorrigible."

Julia hugged her back. "Does that mean you'll stay?"

"You bet your life I will. Someone has to keep an eye on you."

The End

Thank you for reading, *You Bet Your Life*, the first book in the Willows Bend Cozy Mysteries Series. If you enjoyed it, please leave a review on Amazon. **Reviews needn't be long, but they really do make a difference.**

Other Novels by Evelyn Cullet:

The Charlotte Ross Mysteries:

Love, Lies and Murder

Masterpiece of Murder

Once Upon a Crime

The Tarkington Treasure

The Willows Bend Cozy Mysteries

You Bet Your Life

The Crone's Curse

About the Author

Evelyn Cullet has been an author since high school when she wrote short stories. She began her first novel while attending college later in life, and while working in the offices of a major soft drink company. Now, with early retirement, she finally has the chance to do what she loves best: write full time. As a life-long mystery buff, she was a former member of the Agatha Christie Society, and is a current member of the National Chapter of Sisters In Crime. When she's not writing mysteries, reading them or reviewing them, she hosts other authors and their work on her writer's blog, www.evelyncullet.com/blog. She also plays the piano, is an amateur lapidary, and an organic gardener.

Made in the USA
Las Vegas, NV
03 January 2023

64669115R00138